Emoji

A Harry Starke Novel

By

Blair Howard

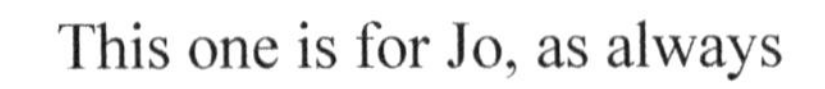
This one is for Jo, as always

Prologue

He'd been waiting almost thirty minutes when she finally came out of the two-story house on Oak Street. Long enough to make him nervous about being spotted, but then again, so what if he was seen? He had every right to be on the UTC campus. But nerves were to be expected; he was human, after all. He smiled. No, he wasn't human. Not even close. Even he knew that.

She trotted down the steps, arms bent at the elbows, hands in front of her and closed into fists, like a professional boxer. She wore a black tank top and red athletic shorts. Her hair was tied back in a ponytail.

Mmmm, she looks good. Running a little late, but that's not a problem.

She stopped at the curb, glanced down the street in both directions, then trotted across, headed in the direction of the Palmetto parking lot and her Honda Civic, just as he knew she would. He should. He'd been watching her for weeks.

He was parked facing the way he knew she would run, the passenger side window already down.

"Hey Maggie!" he shouted as she drew alongside. "You going to the Riverpark?"

Of course she is. She always does.

She stopped, looked in through the window, smiled, placed her elbows on the sill and said, "You know I am. Are you?"

He was dressed for it: shorts, T-shirt, sneakers.

"Yeah. You want a ride? We can run together and then I can bring you back?" He held his breath while she considered the offer.

Then she shrugged. "Sure. Why not."

He smiled. She opened the door and got in. He put the car in gear and….

Chapter 1

It had been almost two months since I'd gotten out of the hospital. Two months since Amanda killed Calaway Jones. Neither or us had quite recovered from it, but for different reasons. She had never killed anyone before, and I'd never come as close to being killed myself as I had that day. If Amanda hadn't… if I hadn't… if… if… if…. As it was, I'm told it was pretty much a toss-up whether I lived or died.

I'd survived the confrontation with the Mossad assassin, but barely. I spent the first thirty-eight hours in an induced coma—that, plus a badly fractured left arm, two broken ribs, several serious lacerations, and a hairline fracture to my skull. Lucky? Yes, you could say that.

You've seen it happen in movies, right, when the hero is rescued in the nick of time? It never happens in real life though, does it? That's what I thought too, but it happened to me. Amanda and Tim burst in just as Calaway was about to finish me off.

Amanda is, in some ways, tougher than I am. On that day two months later, she was at work, at Channel 7 TV, as an anchor, doing what she loves to do. Me? Not so much. The cast had been taken off my arm a couple weeks earlier, and the arm was still in a brace but I could do some stuff, sort of, even though it still hurt like hell at times. But my problems were more psychological than physical. When you come as close to death as I had, something happens inside, something it's tough to come to grips with—at least for me it has been. I'm not going to tell you I had any memories of my near-death experience. I didn't. There was no light at the end of the tunnel, no out-of-body experience, just… nothing. I awoke almost two days later remembering only Calaway Jones standing over me, about to deliver the final blow.

It was the realization of just how close I'd come to dying that weighed heavily in my thoughts that day. No, I'm not afraid of death. I just don't think it's prudent to go looking for it… or at it, for that matter. Over the past sixteen years or so I'd seen far too much of it.

One thing I did know for sure was that it was over, the whole private investigator thing. I was done with it. I'm not a cop anymore; I wasn't supposed to get into the kinds of scrapes I'd managed to get myself into over the last three years. Hell, what we do is supposed to be all routine… well, almost all of it: security, white collar crime, legal investigations for attorneys, things like that. Murder and mayhem? Hell no. I'm no Mike Hammer. But over the years I'd seen more death and heartbreak than most people do in two lifetimes, and I'd had it.

D'you have any idea what it does to a man to look down at the body of a six-year-old kid, a girl, who's been tortured to death? No, of course you don't. But I do. How about a young woman in her early twenties, raped repeatedly and then strangled to death? No, of course you don't, but I do, and I could go on and on… but….

On that day, September 4, Labor Day, 2017, I finally made up my mind that I was done with it. I quit.

Well, in my own mind I did.

I was seated on a lounger by the pool at our home on Lookout Mountain. Amanda, as I said, was at work, and I was daydreaming. It was almost noon and I'd been out there since… oh, I dunno… seven thirty, maybe, and I was on what had to be at least my sixth cup of coffee.

It was one of those late summer days that borders on glorious. The temperature was in the low seventies and a cool breeze was blowing across the crest of the mountain and, black as my mood was, I was glad to be alive, and even more so because I realized just how close I'd come to not… er, being alive.

I hadn't told Amanda I was going to quit the agency—but I'm sure she'd gotten the idea—nor had I told Jacque and Bob, my two closest associates. I hadn't told Kate either. But what reasons could they have given me not to do it? I was forty-six years old, didn't need the money or the aggravation, and I sure as hell didn't want to see any more dead bodies. I figured I could do whatever the hell I wanted. I could buy that damned boat if I wanted to—and I did want to. Jacque and Bob could run the business well enough without me, and Kate didn't need me….

No, she could and would have to do it without me. I was done with that life forever.

So when my iPhone vibrated on the table beside me, and I saw who was calling, I ignored it. It rang again; I ignored it. It rang again; I sighed and answered it.

"Yes, Kate, what is it?"

"Why are you ignoring my calls?"

"I'm not… well, yes, I guess I am, and probably with good reason. What do you want?"

"I need your help. I'm at—"

I hung up the phone and turned it off. I knew what she wanted, and I wasn't having any of it. The problem was…. Well, I knew Kate only too well, so I wasn't too surprised when thirty minutes later I heard a car screech to a stop outside the front gate. I sighed, got up out of the lounger, and went to meet her.

"You son of a bitch, Harry. Don't you *ever* hang up on me again. I don't deserve that kind of treatment, especially from you."

"Sure, Kate, come on in. Go sit yourself down by the pool. What would you like to drink? Coffee? Tea?"

"Oh, shut up," she said as she followed me through the house. "I need some help, dammit." She looked me up and down. I must have been quite a sight: unshaven and wearing only boxers and a T-shirt. "And for God's sake go get dressed. You're coming with me."

I grinned at her. "No, Kate, I'm not. So either stay a while, or get the hell out of here."

Her hands went to her hips. She was tall, almost six feet, with a slender figure. Her hair was a tawny blonde, today a bit messy, and her oval face was defined by a high forehead and a pair of huge hazel eyes. As I remember it, she was wearing lightweight tan pants, tan shoes with flat heels, and a white T-shirt under a black leather vest. And, like always, she had a Glock 43 in a holster on her right hip and a gold lieutenant's badge on her left.

"Harry, I'm serious. I need you to come with me. I need your input."

"Nope. I've quit. I'm done with it, Kate. No more. Not ever. Now, coffee or tea? It's a serious question this time."

She stared at me, slowly shaking her head.

I shrugged.

"Quit?" she echoed. "You *quit?* What the hell are you talking about? You can't just... *quit*. What about your business? What about Bob and Jacque and Tim and the others?"

"The business will continue, but without me. They'll manage just fine."

She stared at me, her eyes wide, unbelieving, then finally she said, "Okay, fine. We can talk about it later. Right now I need you. Just come and take a look, please?"

"Nope. Not gonna do it." And then my curiosity got the better of me. "What do you want, anyway?"

"I need you come with me to Doc's—"

"Uh. Nope."

"Look, Harry. I understand how you feel. I mean… no. I actually don't. I understand you've had a rough time, but you've gotta snap out of it. The world hasn't stopped turning since you got hurt."

"Since I got hurt? That's not it, Kate. I've had it. I'm burned out. No more death, rape…. I can't do it anymore; I just can't."

"Okay, so do this for me. Just come with me. Take a look. Tell me what you think, and—"

"And then you'll suck me in, just like you always do. No. Just go. Leave me alone. Get the hell out of here, Kate."

"What's going on?"

I turned around. Amanda was walking across the patio towards us. Surprise. I hadn't heard her car.

"Your husband's being an ass, is what's going on," Kate said, turning to her.

"She wants me to go visit another damned dead body, and I'm not going to do it. I'm through with all that. I've decided to quit."

"*What?*" Amanda asked. "What are you talking about?"

"What I said. I quit. I'm done. It's over. In the past. Umm… how can I make it any plainer?" I was getting angry. "I friggin' *quit.* I am *finished* with it."

"Oh for God's sake don't be stupid. You can't quit, and if Kate needs your help, you'll do it. She's done enough for you over the years." She turned to Kate. "The body they found this morning?"

Amanda works for Channel 7 TV. She's a news anchor.

Kate's eyes narrowed. She didn't look happy, but she nodded.

"I thought so," Amanda said. "We have a team covering it. Can I ask…." She saw the look on Kate's face. "No, I guess not."

She turned her attention back to me. "For God's sake go get dressed… and take a shower… and shave that mess off your face. You look like a hobo."

I looked at them, from one to the other and then back again.

Amanda is a strikingly beautiful woman in her mid-thirties: tall, strawberry blonde, with a heart-shaped face and high cheekbones, a small, slightly upturned nose, and wide-set, jade-green eyes. She was dressed for work in a red blazer over a white dress. She wasn't angry, I could tell, but she wasn't in any mood to take no for an answer either.

The two of them together were a formidable pair, and I knew I wasn't going to win. I did as I was told.

Thirty minutes later Kate and I were headed down Lookout Mountain to Amnicola Highway, where Dr. Richard Sheddon, Hamilton County's Chief Medical Examiner, ruled over the small forensic center.

And there's another fine character for you. Doc's not exactly a ghoul, but I sometimes wonder if he wouldn't have been happier living among the undead. That man loves his job, that's for sure. I once asked him why he did it, why he decided to become a pathologist. His answer: "My patients never complain."

He's a small man, a little overweight, almost totally bald and with a round face—Chattanooga's own Bilbo Baggins. Most of the time he's a jovial little man, but not that day.

"Hello, Harry. How you feeling? Better, I hope." He sounded tired, depressed even, and that augured no good news, I was sure. "Kate managed to talk you into it then? I didn't think she would."

During the ride down the mountain, I had tried to get Kate to tell me what it was all about, but she wouldn't discuss it. That didn't sit well with me. And now this….

Doc wasn't exactly dressed for work—he had his suit jacket off and his sleeves rolled up—but as he turned and walked down the corridor to the place I dreaded most on this earth, he beckoned and sighed.

"Suit up," he said, handing us white Tyvek coveralls. "You'll have to join me."

He slipped on a lab coat and, without waiting for us, pushed through the doors into the autopsy room.

"Jeez, Kate," I said. "What the hell are we doing here?"

She didn't answer. She didn't need to. I already knew the answer. Even so, I wasn't prepared for what I saw next.

Doc Sheddon took a position at the far side of the autopsy table, his hands in the pockets of his lab coat, his chin on his chest, and stared down at the corpse stretched out before him on the stainless steel table. Kate and I stood together on the other side of the table. And boy was I pissed off.

Carol Oats, Doc's resident forensic anthropologist, had tried to provide the girl with some modesty. A white towel had been folded lengthwise and laid across her breasts; another covered her hips. It was a nice thought, but it did little to hide the results of Doc's invasive procedures.

The atmosphere in that room—the mood, call it what you will—was dismal. Sheddon, usually a chattering mine of gallows humor as he worked, was glum. Carol—or Bones, as Doc Sheddon insisted on calling her—wore a bleak look, and Kate's face was white.

Me? My guts were churning. I was furious. This was exactly what I hadn't wanted to see ever again.

"Carol's just finished cleaning her up," Sheddon said. He removed his hands from his pockets and placed them on the edge of the table. "We're done with her."

She was thin, and looked very young, no more than or sixteen or seventeen years old. She lay face up on the gleaming table. The skin of her legs, chest, and face was already discolored—she was in the early stages of putrefaction.

Most of Doc's classic Y incision was visible. The section at the girl's breasts was covered by the towel. The rest, from the shoulder joints to the pubic area, was a sight that would turn even a strong man's stomach, and mine was no exception.

"Female," Sheddon began. "Caucasian, late teens to early twenties, somewhat underweight, healthy, probably from a wealthy family—no tattoos or piercings, teeth in perfect alignment…."

He trailed off, seemingly lost in thought.

"There are some sick bastards out there," he said eventually. He looked up, stared at me.

Here it comes, I thought, and gritted my teeth.

"The cause of death is manual strangulation, but… well, more about that in a minute. Time of death… two days ago… maybe two and a half. There was no identifiable gastric material in her stomach, which means that when she died she hadn't eaten for at least three days. Rigor has passed. The skin is showing some marbling and there's livor mortis present—lividity—in the buttocks, ankles, and feet, but none in the face, chest, back, or shoulders. That's unusual but, considering the circumstances, understandable."

He looked up at me. I stared across the table at him. I didn't need to ask what he meant. He'd tell me.

He shrugged, leaned forward and placed his hands on the edge of the table, and looked down at the girl's face. He took a deep breath and said, "She was found sitting under a tree. Lividity is fixed. That usually takes about twelve hours. So she must have been posed in that position shortly after death; within one or two hours. Given the condition of the body, I'd say she died sometime between eight o'clock on Friday evening and eight on Saturday morning. That's as close as I can get it. I'd say, however, that she hadn't been under that tree very long before she was found. That means she was killed somewhere else."

"You said she was strangled?" Kate asked.

He didn't look up from the girl's face, "I did, and nastily too. She was strangled almost to the point of death several times, maybe many times, then resuscitated. The bruising to her neck is extensive. Petechial hemorrhaging is present in the face, eyes, and eyelids, and there is cyanosis present at the lips, nose, and fingernails. This kid was put through hell." He paused, folded his arms.

"When the carotid arteries or the jugular veins are subjected to heavy pressure, it renders the victim unconscious in just a few seconds. Release that pressure, and consciousness returns in about ten seconds. And that, I think, is what we have here. But that's not all. The larynx and hyoid are also crushed, which takes a lot of pressure, and if the pressure was applied as slowly as I think…." He shook his head as if to rid himself of the image. "This girl suffered terribly. Somebody played with her—" he stared down at her face, blinked "—over the course of two or three days.

"And there are other injuries," he continued. "Her eyes were taped open and she was restrained: head, hands, and feet. There are ligature marks on her wrists and ankles. The marks on her forehead were caused by some sort of tape that was used to hold her head still—duct tape, I think, judging from the damage to the skin. She was probably stretched out on some sort of bench or table and immobilized." Again, he lowered his chin to his chest and closed his eyes, took a deep breath, and opened them again.

"There are both external and internal injuries to the vagina," he continued, "but I won't go into detail; I'm sure you get the idea."

Oh shit, I thought. *I don't need this.*

"As for trace evidence, DNA," Doc continued, "I found very little. The body had been washed, inside and out. If there was semen, it's gone. There are even traces of bleach inside her, so it was a thorough cleansing. I found a couple of human hairs.

They could be hers, or not. We'll see. I also found a single brown synthetic fiber in her hair. What it's from I have no idea. Maybe a carpet or rug, maybe something else. All of it will need to be analyzed. And… well, that's about it, at least for now. The tox screen, the hair and fiber analysis, that could take a couple of weeks. The cause of death, however, I can say with certainty was asphyxia caused by manual strangulation."

"Do we know who she is?" Kate asked.

"No. Not yet."

I stared down at the ruined remains of the young girl and felt physically sick. My head swam. It was Emily Johnston, Chief Johnston's daughter, all over again. Oh Emily was a little older, but still a kid as far as I was concerned, and here it was—deja vu all over again. *Shit, shit, shit.*

"Jesus Christ. Why am I here, Kate?" I asked. "This is a homicide. I don't do those anymore."

"You know why. This isn't LA or New York. We're a small department and I'm slammed; I have a dozen homicides on my plate and this is not a routine case. I need help, qualified help. I need you. You were a homicide detective for eight years, Harry. There is no one else."

"For Christ's sake, call in the TBI instead. FBI, GBI, the damned Sheriff, whatever, get some outside help. I can't do it. I just can't…."

She sighed, looked hard at me, then said, "I don't *want* to call in outside help. You know what a damn circus it always turns into. And there's more, Harry. She isn't the first. There are two more."

She stared at me through those damned great long eyelashes.

My heart sank. I knew what was coming and I didn't want to hear it. "Don't, Kate. Please, just leave me alone, okay?" And I turned and walked out, leaving them staring after me. I felt like shit, but I couldn't help it. I'd had enough.

I was all the way out to the parking lot before I realized I didn't have a ride home, so I went back inside and asked Kate to take me to my office on Georgia Avenue. I'd get someone there to take me home.

She drove me to Georgia without saying a word. I didn't say anything either. She dropped me off, then she drove away; she didn't even say goodbye. I didn't blame her.

Chapter 2

It was after two o'clock that afternoon when I walked into the office, and I was struck by how quiet it was. I hadn't been inside those doors in almost two months, not since the day Calaway Jones almost put out my lights for good.

Jacque, Heather, and the girls were going about their various tasks, but Jacque started to her feet when she saw me. I waved her down again.

"Don't bother," I said. "I'm not staying. I just need a ride home. I thought maybe Leslie or Margo...."

"I'll do it," Bob said, walking out of one of the back offices.

"Hey," I said. "No. One of... oh hell, okay. Let's go." And I turned to leave.

"Just you wait one damn minute." There it was: that damned Jamaican accent Jacque used when she was pissed. I turned again to face her.

"Jacque...."

"Don't. Don't say it. What you t'ink you doin' comin' in here and don't even say hello? You bin gone two mont's an' you got nothin' to say to us?"

I heaved a sigh, looked around at their grim faces, shook my head, then said, brightly, "Coffee, anyone?"

A few minutes later we—Jacque, Bob, and I—were seated around the coffee table in my private office. It had been so long since anyone had used it that it smelt slightly musty, and it felt empty—abandoned, almost, as I suppose it had been. As much as I loved my inner sanctum, I didn't feel comfortable there. It was… unsettling.

"What's going on, Harry?" Bob asked quietly. "When are you coming back to work?"

I leaned back in my chair, cradled my mug in both hands, put my head back, and stared up at the ceiling.

"I don't know," I said at last. "Maybe never."

"Bullshit. That's a crock if ever I heard one. You couldn't live without this place."

"Hah. You think?"

"Yeah. You've gotta snap out of it, Harry. Amanda called me this morning. She's worried about you, man… and so am I."

What do you say to that? I couldn't think of anything, so I said nothing. I just sipped on my coffee and waited. My mood was one of… I couldn't really care less. I loved those people, and I felt their love for me, but I was indifferent to it. My mind was… not exactly a blank, but it was sure as hell close to it. I just didn't care anymore.

"Harry," Jacque said quietly, "we need you. We can't do this without you. You…. What?"

I was shaking my head. "You're going to have to."

"Harry, what the hell is wrong with you?" Bob asked. "So you got a bang on the head, you got hurt. No big deal. You've gotten over it. Now for God's sake, get with program and come on back. Jacque's right. We can't do this without you. Clients are complaining. They don't want us. They want you. *We* want you. All of us."

I looked at them, stared at them, said nothing, and then Jacque did something I would not have thought she was capable of. She got up from her seat, came around the table, crouched down in front of me, and took both my hands in hers.

"Please, Harry." She looked up at me, halfway to tears, pleading. "Please come back."

I leaned forward, kissed her cheek, and said, "I don't know, Jacque. Give me a little time. I'll think about it." And then I rose to my feet, dropped her hands, and left them there staring after me.

Think about it? Hah. I don't need to think about it. I'm done with it. They can have it. I'll have August draw up the papers tomorrow and gift the business to Jacque and Bob.

I had Lori, the company's intern, drive me home. I didn't know her all that well, so I had no fears of unwanted conversation.

By four o'clock that afternoon I was swimming laps, working on my injured arm. It was stiff. The hand was fine; the wrist and elbow were not, but they were getting there. I just needed to keep exercising it. Swimming, I figured, was as good a way as any, and swimming helped in another way too. It had a calming effect.

Later that evening, much later, I was still out on the patio but now with a half-empty bottle of

Scotland's finest. I was, as they say, feeling no pain—for the first time in more than two months.

It was a cool, clear night. The sky was a field of glittering stars and the half moon that hung over the city seemed too big to be real. It dominated the sky and turned the river below into a glistening ribbon of silver that meandered back and forth until finally it disappeared into the distance. The city itself was a vast, jeweled carpet of red, orange, and gold. It was easy to image it might have been thrown down by some giant hand. Whatever. It too had a calming effect on what I realize now was my troubled soul.

I gazed up at the night sky, as I often did. Orion was above the crest of the mountain to the south, the Seven Sisters almost overhead to the north. I gazed up at Orion's Belt and wondered what it was like up there. It's hard to believe that the nearest star is more than eight hundred light years away, the farthest more than thirteen hundred.

Yeah, I was lost alright—away with the birds, gone, in another world. No, not drunk; far from it. Feeling sorry for myself? Perhaps. Anyway, around 11:45 I heard Amanda's car arrive and the gate open and then the garage door. On any other day I would have jumped up and gone to meet her, but I stayed put. I knew she'd come and find me, and she did, but not before she changed into a swimsuit.

She said not a word. Didn't even look at me. She dove into the pool, swam several laps, then rested her forearms on the infinity wall, looking out at the city. I knew what she was doing. She was preparing herself.

She turned her head, looked at me, smiled, then swam to the steps and rose from the water like some Greek goddess, her head tilted downward a little, her hair plastered against her forehead and ears, and she came to me. She sat down on my lap, water streaming from her body, droplets on her skin glistening in the moonlight. She wrapped her arms around my neck and lay down on top of me. I put a finger under her chin and lifted her head. Her face was wet, but not all of it was from the pool; she was crying.

"Hey," I said gently. "What is it?"

She just shook her head and laid her cheek down again on my chest. And there she stayed for a long time. Finally, she stood and left me. She'd been home for more than an hour and she hadn't said a word. That got to me. It hit me hard.

By the time I'd dried myself off and gone into the house she was in bed, her eyes closed. Asleep? I never found out. The lecture I'd been expecting never happened. Well, not that night anyway.

It was one of the worst nights of my life. I dreamed… no, I had nightmares. I was back in Doc Sheddon's house of horror. The girl was still lying on the stainless steel table. The sutures that held together that godawful Y incision were red from the blood seeping from the wound—yeah, I know dead people don't bleed—and her face was a deep blue-violet, the result of asphyxia. In the dream I leaned over the body, brushed her cheek with the back of my hand. She was ice cold. I leaned in closer to kiss her forehead. My face was within inches of hers when her eyes snapped open.

"Help… me… please," she gasped. No, not a gasp, more of a wheeze that seemed to come from deep within her, from the lungs I knew she no longer possessed. I started back, away from her… and then I woke up sweating, the pillow and sheets soaked.

I sat up in bed, stared up into the black corners of the ceiling, and there it was, the beast of my childhood, the black, undulating, oozing thing I used to watch after my mother left me alone in the dark.

I looked down at Amanda. She was asleep, breathing gently. I looked at the clock. It was a little after two. I got up and went to the bathroom. When I returned, I sat down on the edge of the bed and looked again into the darkened corner of the ceiling. Nothing. The monster was gone, but the nightmare vision of the murdered girl remained, vivid, demanding, and I had a feeling that she was going to haunt me until I could put her to rest… and suddenly, I knew what I had to do.

Chapter 3

I rose early that morning. I'd slept only fitfully after returning to bed, but I felt good, really good. I dressed in running gear and headed out along East Brow at a fast jog. Most mornings I'd run a couple of miles, but that day I ran almost to Covenant College and back, more than seven miles. When I returned, Amanda was already drinking her first cup of coffee. I went to her and kissed her good morning. She smiled up at me. I told her I'd be a few minutes, that I needed a shower. When I returned some fifteen minutes later wrapped in a towel, she already had coffee waiting for me. I sipped it gratefully. We sat together for several minutes, neither of us saying a word, but I've come to know her well over the past few years and knew what was about to come. And it did.

She laid her cup down on the breakfast bar and took my hand. "What are we going to do, Harry?"

I squeezed her hand, smiled at her, leaned in, kissed her gently on the lips, and then leaned back again. "It's okay," I said. "I'm over it. I'm going into the office this morning."

The light came on in her eyes and she leaped off the stool, wrapped her arms around my neck, and squeezed me half to death. Then she kissed me, and there was nothing gentle about it. Something stirred inside me. Desire? Yes, but something more. We hadn't made love since… well, we just hadn't, but that morning we did, and it was amazing. When I climbed into the Beast—my Camaro ZL1—just before eight and headed down the mountain toward the city, I felt like a kid again. Something—and I could only believe it was the girl in my dream—had handed me back my life, and it felt good. I felt good.

I had a killer to find.

Chapter 4

My appearance in the office that morning was, to say the least, unexpected. The welcome I received from my crew was also… unexpected. I was treated like a conquering hero home from the wars, not the washed up ex-cop I really was. Jacque was actually *crying*, something I don't think I'd ever seen before. Bob? Well, he was Bob. As always he gave little away, other than that big stupid grin of his. And it was happy smiles and kind words from everyone else, too.

Tuesday wasn't the usual day for our meeting—that was always on Fridays—but needs must, as they say. I had everyone assemble in the conference room, and took my place on the throne at the head of the table.

"Okay," I said when everyone was seated. "What do we have working? More to the point, Jacque, you mentioned yesterday that we're losing clients. Tell me about it."

"Harry, it's been slow since you left. We cleared most of what was on the books when you… when… well, you know. Right now we have five active cases and one or two small inquiries and… well, we're just wrapping them up too. Clients call, but they ask for you. They ask when you'll be back. We had no answers so…. I told you, Harry, the clients want you. That's the way it is. Another three weeks like the last and we'll be closing the doors."

"No! Not going to happen." I looked at them all in turn; the worry was plain to see on their faces. "Don't worry," I said. "Everything will be fine."

"How can it be fine? We have no money coming in."

"That's okay," I said. "I can cover the expenses until things get moving again. In the meantime, contact all of our regular clients and let them know I'm back at work. Bob? What do you have going?"

"Not much. Just a routine investigation for Larry Spruce and a divorce case that will be wrapped up in a couple of days."

I nodded. Larry Spruce is the senior ADA in Chattanooga and we do a lot of work for his office; he's also a close friend of mine and a golfing buddy, though we haven't played since before Calaway Jones.

"Tim," I said. "How about you?" Tim's my resident computer geek. If he has nothing to do, he'll make something.

"I have a hacking thing I'm looking into."

And so it went for about half an hour, until I'd had enough of it. I hadn't come back to get involved in the day-to-day drag of the office.

"Okay," I said. "That's enough. Jacque, you can handle all of nitty gritty stuff, yeah?"

She nodded. "Just make sure you contact all of the clients and get things moving again."

I nodded. "I think we're done here, then. Jacque, Bob, I need a word. The rest of you can go about your day.

"Okay," I said after the room had cleared. "I don't know what my place here is, or what it's going to be…." I could see Jacque was about to interrupt me, and I lifted a hand. "No, no, let me finish. I don't know what my place is here, but for sure I don't want to be involved in the day-to-day running of the business. Jacque, I want you to handle that; you and Bob. In return, I intend to make you both partners. I'll retain ownership of fifty-two percent of the company. You get twenty-four percent each. If that sounds good to you two, I'll have August draw up the paperwork. Yeah?"

They were stunned.

"But… but why?" Jacque asked. "What are you…."

"Look, I told you all yesterday that I wanted out, and to a certain extent that's still true. I don't need the money and I certainly don't need…. Look, I've been shot several times, beaten within an inch of my life, and dealt with more death and heartache than anyone deserves. And I… well, I won't beat a dead horse. Having said that, I've come to realize that it's part of who I am, and always will be. So what do you say? Are you in or out?"

They sat for a moment, staring at me, then at each other, then again at me, until finally Bob cleared his throat and said, "Harry, are you sure this is what you want?"

I nodded.

Bob looked at Jacque. She shrugged and nodded. Bob grinned, stood, reached across the table, and offered me his hand.

"Yeah, partner, I'm in. What's it going to cost me?"

"One dollar. Jacque? How about you?"

She stood, walked around the end of the table, and hugged me. "Yes, me too. Thank you, Harry." Then she kissed my forehead and turned quickly toward the door.

"Hey wait, come back. I'm not done yet."

She was already at the doorway, but she stopped, and I saw her wipe her eyes, then she turned, sat back down at the table, sniffed, and started laughing.

"Oh man," she said, wiping her eyes with the backs of her hands again. "You are so full of shit and surprises."

"Don't get carried away," I said. "It's not that big of a deal. Your salaries will stay the same, but both of you will get your percentage of the profits each year too." I paused, grinned, then said lightly, "If there are any. And that's now up to you two. But as far as the clients are concerned, I'm back and nothing has changed." I grinned at them.

"Now," I said, leaning back in my chair and linking my fingers at the back of my neck, "with that out of the way, you're probably wondering what changed my mind, why I decided to come back."

I looked from Jacque to Bob, then back again. Jacque cocked her head to one side and raised her eyebrows; Bob smiled and said nothing.

"Well I'll tell you then," I said. "Kate—"

"Yeah, we know," Bob said, folding his arms on the table. "She told us. She came back after you left yesterday afternoon. She was upset, which is putting it mildly. I told her to give you a couple of days, and she's waiting for you to call. I'd do it now. She ain't the type you want piss off."

That said, he stood up. "Alright, I have things to do, Harry. So do you, Jacque. Let's leave our new partner to make his call." And they did. They left me sitting there staring after them, shaking my head.

And I thought I *was the smart one!*

It took me a while before I could make the call to Kate. I didn't know what to say to her, much less how to say it. In the end I sighed, dragged my iPhone out of my pocket, and hit the speed dial.

"Hello, Harry." Her voice was cool—not cold, just cool.

"Okay," I said. "I'm sorry."

I heard her sigh. "Well look," she said, "I'm in the incident room, up to my eyes. Are you coming or not?"

"I'll be there in thirty minutes."

"Good. I'll have the front desk buzz you through."

I disconnected and stared down at the screen. *No, it's not that easy. It's never that easy.*

Chapter 5

The incident room had changed very little since I left the department back in 2008. It was an airy, open-plan space on the second floor, overlooking the motor pool at the rear of the building. It wasn't a huge room, maybe fifty feet by thirty, but it was a busy place and obviously being used for at least a half dozen cases at once. Three large tables stacked with papers divided the room in two; a dozen or so desks and double that number of chairs were scattered around, seemingly without much thought or organization. The two end walls were hung with dry erase boards, and three more freestanding, double-sided boards stood at what I assumed to be strategic locations around the room. Kate was sat on the corner of one of the tables on the east side of the room facing one of the free-standing boards; Sergeant Lonnie Guest was seated behind her at an open laptop with a cell phone at his ear. Detective Sarah Foote was seated next to him, reading through a thick stack of forms. Kate spotted me as soon as I walked into the room, and beckoned for me to join them.

As I headed toward her, I was conscious of dozens of pairs of eyes on me. Most of the people here I knew, but a few I didn't. I had no doubt that would change over the next several days.

"Hello Harry," Kate said, as she slid off the table and offered me her hand. "Glad you could make it." It was said with no little sarcasm, which I ignored as I took her hand.

"Glad to be here," I lied as I turned to greet the other two. "Lonnie," I said, grasping his hand. "Sarah. It's been a long time. You doing okay?"

She said she was, and then she and Lonnie resumed their seats and their tasks—the reception, from all three, had been friendly but decidedly cool. Inwardly, I shrugged. Outwardly, I played the enthusiastic newcomer.

"So, Kate," I said, rubbing my hands together. "Talk to me. What do you have?"

Now, you have to understand that Kate and I go back a long way, more than sixteen years, to when she was a rookie cop. She was my partner in the Homicide Division for almost eight years, and much more than that long after I punched my ticket nine years ago.

Since I'd left the PD, we'd remained friends and semi-official partners, an arrangement she had actively fostered, calling me in sometimes as an unpaid consultant. It was an arrangement that was reluctantly sanctioned by her boss and my one-time nemesis, Police Chief Wesley Johnston.

The rivers between Kate and me run deep. There was a time when I might have asked her to marry me but back in the day I was maybe a little too loose with my relationships and… well, she cut the cord. But that was then and, as I said, we'd remained friends. *And here we go again*, I thought, as I looked at the big whiteboard. *Jeez! What the hell was I thinking?*

Someone had drawn three red lines down the board from top to bottom, dividing it into four columns. At the top of each of the first three columns was a group of five or six colored photographs of naked bodies; three different bodies; three girls, although one of them was barely recognizable as such. The fourth column was ominously empty.

"You're expecting more," I said, nodding at the empty space on the board.

Kate shrugged. "Maybe."

I moved closer to the board to get a better look, and immediately wished I hadn't. They were, for the most part, crime scene photos, although there were autopsy images for each as well. It was gruesome, sickening. The one on the right I recognized as the girl from Doc Sheddon's house of horrors; she was obviously the latest addition to the group.

The first girl, the one on the left—identified as Dana Walters—was in a state of advanced decomposition. The lips were gone, the eye sockets empty and devoid of any soft tissue around them; what little skin there was left, was a deep, purplish black.

The second girl, identified as Jasmine Payne, was in only slightly better condition.

The third girl, my girl, the girl with no name, was on the right.

Where were you? I asked her in my head. *Who the hell did this to you? Why? Why? What kind of sick mind can do something like this to a kid?*

I'd seen it all before—many times, too many times—and it never got any easier. You'd think I would have gotten used to it, but I hadn't. Nobody does.

I was lost in thought. Staring up at the image of her face, a close-up taken from above, I imagined her staring up through those taped-open eyes at the face of the sick piece of shit that had done this to her. *How did she feel?* Hell, I couldn't even begin to imagine, and then I wondered, *What did* he *feel as he stared down at her, as he put his thumbs to her throat and... and....* I shook my head, violently trying to erase the image from my brain.

"Harry? *Harry!*"

I snapped out of it, startled, then turned around, away from the ghastly images on the board, and I knew I was sweating. I sat myself down at the table, with the board at my back so I didn't have to look at it.

"Are you okay?" Kate asked.

"Hell no, I'm not okay. I'm f… I feel like shit, but that's not all of it. There are no words to describe how I feel when I look at these kids, but you knew that, didn't you, Kate? You dragged me in front of her body and you used her. You knew how I'd feel, and you used her to reel me in. You're a woman. How the hell do you feel? She's just a kid, for

Christ's sake, probably not even twenty years old. How the hell do you think *she* felt?"

Damn I was angry.

"Yeah," she said. "I did know how you'd feel and yes, I did use her to get to you, but I had to. I need you on this, Harry. I need your mind, your expertise, your insight. Shit—" she waved her hand at the photos on the board behind me "—*they* need you, and the next one needs you, and the one after that. It's what you do. Now get over yourself and let's get to work. Either that or get the hell out of here and out of my way and let *me* get on with it."

By the time she'd finished her voice had risen to a shout, and everyone in the room was watching us.

And I almost did it. I almost got up and walked away. But then I saw something in Kate's eyes I'd never seen before: tears.

My anger subsided. I looked around the room. There was not a smile in the place, and I was the bad guy. Kate was one of their own; I no longer was.

"Wow," I said, shaking my head. "Now I really feel like I'm back at home. Okay, Kate. Point taken. Why don't you bring me up to speed? But first, I need to know about the timeline. When did you get the case?"

"I got this one yesterday when the third girl was found. That was just after eight in the morning. Did you see this?" She pointed to one of the photographs.

Oh yeah, I saw it.

It was a wide shot of the crime scene. The photographer must have been on the riverbank with his back to the water, and I knew just where it was; I'd run along that path many times.

The girl was fully clothed in what I took to be running gear: a black, sleeveless tank, a pair of red Nike shorts, and Nike Air Max shoes. She was seated with her back against a tree, hands in her lap, her chin down. If I hadn't known better, I would have thought she was asleep.

I turned in my seat and nodded. "Who found her?"

"A couple of older women out for a power walk. They noticed her on the way out, thought she was resting. Then, on the way back, they saw that she hadn't moved and stopped to see if she was okay."

"That's the Riverwalk, right? It looks like Doc was right, that she was posed."

"It is. And she was." She turned to a large wall map and pointed to a spot on the riverbank just east of the C. B. Robinson Bridge.

"As you can see, the tree trunk was hiding most of her body. If you even saw her you'd probably think, like those two women did, that she was taking a break, watching the river. I've done it myself."

"And that was at what time?"

"I told you. I got the call at about 8:15."

I nodded slowly. “Which means she must have been placed there at or before dawn. It wouldn’t be difficult. She weighs what, a hundred and ten, hundred and fifteen pounds?” I rose to my feet and went to the map.

“There’s a parking lot here—” I pointed “—about twenty yards from the tree. One man could carry her from here to here easily. Maybe a woman could, too?”

“Yeah. I could do it,” Kate said.

“No you couldn’t,” Lonnie said, “Not with her in that condition. Lividity is set. That means she was posed somewhere else, just after she was killed, maybe in a chair. Hell, Kate, she could have been stiff when she was dumped.”

“No, I don’t think so,” Kate replied. “If rigor mortis had set in it would have taken more than one person to carry her. If Doc was right about the TOD, and I wouldn’t bet against him, by the time she was dumped she would have passed through the rigor stage, and that would mean she’d been dead at least thirty-six hours—more, in fact. That would fit with Doc’s estimate. A man or a strong woman could have carried her those twenty-odd yards and set her up against the tree easily enough. Like I said, I could have done it.”

“Have you talked to them yet, the women who found her?” I asked.

“Yes, of course. They found her. That’s it. They didn’t see anything.”

I nodded. “Do we know who she is yet?”

"No. We're waiting for Missing Persons now."

"Forensics?"

She shook her head. "We're still waiting for the report from Mike Willis, but I'm not holding my breath. From what I saw, the area around the body was pristine. The grass had been mowed the day before."

I stepped backward and sat on the edge of the table, staring up at the map, then at the photographs.

"It's a good spot," I said. "Whoever dumped her there wanted her to be found, but not too quickly. Setting her with her back to the tree like that was well thought out, probably decided on well in advance." I nodded to myself, my mind churning. *There's a message here. What the hell is it? If he wanted her found, why semi-hide her like that? Why not just dump her on the riverbank and be done with it?*

"It would be a bit risky though, don't you think?" Lonnie asked, resting his chin on his fists and staring up at the photo. "That's a busy walk. He could have been seen."

"Not if he was careful," Kate said. "If he dropped her off before dawn, and he must have, it would have been deserted, and the field of view from the parking lot is unrestricted. He would have been able to see if anyone was approaching. We're talking what? Sixty seconds, ninety? It wouldn't have been difficult."

And then it was quiet. We stared at the photographs, each with our own thoughts, and then I broke the spell.

"Okay," I said. "The other two. Tell me about them."

Kate nodded. "This girl, Dana Walters." She tapped the top photo in the first column. "She died some twelve months ago, according to the doc. She was dumped in a wooded gully that runs parallel to Volkswagen Drive, here, just west of the I-75 off ramp. She was found by a road crew back in March. As you can see she was in the final stages of decomposition, almost skeletonized. Cause of death was strangulation; the hyoid bone was crushed and she was dumped in a ditch and covered with leaves. She wasn't found until almost six months later."

"Jasmine Payne," Kate said, turning to look at her, "was in far better shape than the first victim, as you can see. Much like the third, she was dumped where she could be found, though, and she wasn't posed. She was also found on the Riverwalk, right here." Again, she pointed to a spot on the map. I knew it well. "Under the railway bridge."

"Who found her?" I asked.

"One of the city employees did, when he was mowing. She was lying near the steel support column and invisible from the walk. She was behind one of those huge bridge stanchions. Not exactly hidden, but out of sight, if you know what I mean. And she was strangled, multiple times."

I nodded. "When was she found?"

"July fifteenth, a Saturday. Seven weeks ago, give or take. Doc estimated the time of death to be about three days earlier, on the twelfth, between six in the evening and six the following morning."

"Okay," I said, shifting on the edge of the table. "Now for the big one. What makes you think they're connected?"

I thought I already knew the answer, but I wanted to hear her tell it.

She gave that look. You know the one. It said, *Are you kidding me?* "The cause of death, Harry. They were all strangled, two of them multiple times. Maybe the first one too, but she was too decomposed to tell for sure. And then there's where the bodies were found, and the age of the girls. They're all young and, although Dana Walters wasn't found on the Riverwalk, she was dumped on the right side of town. Finally, the first two girls were attending UTC." She paused, looked at the board, then continued. "It's escalating, Harry. Time and method."

"So you're thinking we have a serial killer then? What does the chief think?"

"I think she's right."

I jerked upright, turned to face him. I hadn't heard him enter the room.

I hadn't seen much of Wesley Johnston since his daughter went missing almost two years ago. He never seemed to change much. Certainly he hadn't aged any. He was a big man; not fat, well built with a chest like a barrel and a big, round head that he kept shaved and polished to a shine. His signature Hulk Hogan mustache seemed bigger than ever, and was white as snow.

Does he bleach that thing? I wondered.

His uniform was crisp—not a wrinkle in the pants, the shirt starched and pressed as a marine's. He had an air about him, not of arrogance but of authority; he was used to things being done his way, and he expected total obedience from his underlings. He was, as they say, larger than life.

Back in the day, when I worked for him, we didn't often see eye-to-eye; just the opposite in fact. He tolerated me… and the way I worked, only because I was able to get the job done, and it was me he came to when Emily, his daughter, went missing… but that's a whole 'nother story.

He held out his hand for me to shake. I took it.

"It's good see you again, Harry. Are you fully recovered from… from your little altercation?"

Little altercation? Hell, you should have been there.

"Ah, mostly," I said. "I still have a few twinges in my arm… but yeah."

"Good." He nodded. "So you're in on this, right?"

"Yes… but don't you think you should call in the TBI? They have the resources to handle something like this. You—"

“Let’s not talk about that,” he butted in. “Not yet anyway. I don’t want them or the feds crawling around all over the place, acting like they’re God’s gift to law enforcement. I think Lieutenant Gazzara has what it takes to handle it, and with you backing her up… well, I think the TBI would be hard pressed to come up with a better team. Kate will lead the investigation; you, my friend, will consult. You’ll have full access but… hmmm, how should I put this?” He looked hard at me. “Play it by the book, Harry. Play by the rules.”

Flattery will get you everywhere you….

He turned to Kate. “I can let you have two more detectives,” he said, “along with Sergeant Guest here. Detective Foote will be one of them, and I’ll leave it to you to choose the other. If you need some uniforms, check with Captain Harker. I’ll give him the word. That’s it. That’s all I can spare.”

“I’ll take Holtz,” she said, “if that’s okay with Jeffrey.”

She was talking about another old nemesis of mine, Ron Jeffrey. There was a day when… and, well, that too is another story. Maybe one for the future.

He nodded. “I’ll square it away with Lieutenant Jeffrey. Any idea where he is?”

“He was here earlier,” Kate said.

“Well, leave Holtz and Jeffrey to me,” Johnston said. “I’ll have Tommy join you ASAP. Keep me posted, Lieutenant. I want to know what’s going on at all times. Capiche?”

"Yes sir."

He nodded at me. "Harry," he said, and then turned and left the room.

I knew Tommy Holtz, but not well. He'd just graduated from the academy when I turned in my resignation. He was maybe thirty years old, a tall, skinny guy with a shock of red hair. I hadn't seen him since I left the PD almost ten years ago.

Why did she pick him, I wonder?

Kate looked at me. "He's smart," she said, "smarter than most."

I tilted my head and smiled.

"What?" she asked.

"How did you know what I was thinking?"

"Harry, you're an open book. I saw the look you gave the chief when I said his name. Tommy's good; he sees thing differently."

"He doesn't change much, does he?" I asked her.

It was Lonnie who answered. "The chief? Friggin' old goat. He needs to put in his papers and go somewhere warm and lie on a beach."

"What did he do to deserve that?"

Kate said, "Lonnie passed the LT exam almost a year ago. He's been passed over twice since then. He thinks the chief has a grudge."

Lonnie passed the lieutenant's exam? Whoa! Now that's something I never thought I'd see. They must have lowered the bar… a lot.

"Hey, Lonnie," I said, grinning at him, "congratulations. That's terrific."

He gave me that same old shit-eating grin I hated and shrugged, but said nothing.

I've known Lonnie ever since we were at the police academy together. Back then he hated my guts, because I'd had no trouble with the academy and he'd had a tough time of it. I'd always wondered how he'd managed to make it through at all, much less pass the final exam. Then I found out his cousin was the mayor.

His Honor lost the election some nine years ago, though, so Lonnie lost his crutch. The mayor's last act was to have Lonnie promoted to sergeant, so yeah, maybe Chief Johnston did have a problem with Lonnie. Well, all of that was no concern of mine. It had taken a lot of years, but Lonnie and I had become friends, sort of, though I didn't trust him, not even a little bit. I had a deep-seated feeling that he'd organized Little Billy Harper's demise. True, the bastard deserved what he got, but… well….

"Maybe the next opening, huh?" I said to Lonnie.

He nodded. The grin was gone. He shuffled the photographs on the table in front of him, then leaned back in his chair and contemplated the ones on the board—or at least he seemed to.

"So let's talk about…" I glanced at the name of the first girl, "Dana Walters. Tell me about her."

Again, it was Lonnie who answered. He flipped through the screens on his iPad and began.

"She was uncovered, literally, just off VW Drive by three guys picking up litter—they were DUIs, drunks doing community service. She was naked, lying face up, partially covered by a layer of rotted leaves. It's thought that whoever dumped her probably covered her up some, and the rest of debris that was on her was the result of the natural progression of the season. Animals caused some damage—the fingers and toes were missing—but other than that the corpse was pretty intact, if almost completely decomposed. Date of death was estimated by a guy from UT Knoxville, a forensic entomologist—" he flipped through his notes "—named Jason Wu. Identity was established primarily through dental records and then confirmed by a DNA match with her mother; her father was deceased." He looked at me and then at Kate, who nodded, so he continued.

"She was reported missing on the morning of October eighth, a Saturday, by her roommate Natalie Gibson. Natalie stated that Dana had gone to the library the previous Friday evening… that would be… the seventh, and she didn't return. A search was instituted but nothing came of it and nothing else was done until her body turned up almost six months later.

"There was an investigation, but after six weeks of nothing, it went cold. And no, Harry," he said as he saw I was about to ask a question, "her death wasn't connected to the second one, not then. She had been forgotten for a long time when Jasmine Payne's body was discovered. It wasn't until this last one was discovered—" he waved his hand in the general direction of the photos on the board "—that Kate put all three together, but she can explain that better than me."

I looked at Kate.

She shrugged. "It was simple enough. I was already the lead working the Jasmine Payne investigation and it was going nowhere. I'd put it on the shelf hoping something would turn up, but there was nothing until…. When this latest body turned up I had Lonnie go back through the missing persons files. That brought up Dana Walters. I figured all three might be connected. I still do… and… well, I'm wondering if there are more girls waiting to be discovered. Comments, Harry?"

I shrugged, thought about it, then said, "The second one, Jasmine Payne. Tell me about her."

"Much the same as the first," Kate said. "She went out on a Monday evening to meet some friends at Starbucks on Hamilton Place Boulevard, to chat and study. She never made it."

"Who reported her missing?" I asked. "And when?"

"Her roommate, Annie Lister, the following morning, Tuesday the thirteenth."

I nodded. "So," I said, "If these girls are connected in some way, why hasn't this latest one been reported missing?"

"Maybe she has. We're still waiting for Missing Persons to answer the call."

"Don't you think it might be a good idea to give 'em a poke, for God's sake? It's been… what." I looked at my watch. "Thirty hours since she was discovered?"

She nodded and looked at Lonnie, who picked up the phone and punched the speed dial. He listened, nodded, listened some more, scribbled something on a legal pad, then said, "I got it, Jim." And then he slowly put the phone back in its cradle and looked first at Kate, then at me, his face grim.

"A girl. Twenty years old, a sophomore at UTC, was reported missing at 12:05 a.m., on the thirtieth. She left her room at 6:15 to go for a run on the Riverwalk. That was the last time she was seen. Her name's Margaret Hart. She's a local girl from Cleveland—well, McDonald, not more than twenty-five miles from here. She… fits the description."

I stared at him. Kate stared at him.

"That was more than five days ago," Kate said, finally. "Doc said our girl died either late evening on the first of September or in the early morning of the second. If she's the missing girl. That means whoever abducted her kept her alive for at least two days, maybe three."

Lonnie nodded. "Sergeant Kearney is faxing the report over now. I'll go get it." And he did.

Five minutes later he was back from the machine with several sheets of paper in his hand. He handed the copy of the report to Kate. She read it over briefly, then handed it to me.

The missing girl was Margaret Hart, twenty years old. She'd been reported missing by her sister, who she lived with. She'd been wearing red running shorts, a black tank with a black sports bra under it, and Nike Air Max shoes.

Oh yeah, it's her. Damn. Dammit.

I threw the papers down on the table and went to the coffee pot. Not that I needed coffee. I just needed to get away for a minute. But I did get coffee, black and thick and old as it was; I poured myself half a cup and carried it back to the table.

Kate looked up as I sat. She was looking over the report again, her eyebrows raised, and she nodded to me, then turned to Detective Foote and said, "I need you to go and bring the sister to the Forensic Center." She handed Foote the report. "Here. We'll meet you there, so call me when you're on the way. Don't tell her too much."

Foote nodded, got to her feet, and left the room. I sat and watched her go, then I stared at the door, then down into my cup at the thick, greasy black coffee.

"Margaret Hart," Kate said, "if it *is* her, is—was an art major at UT. She'd have been back at school for less than two weeks when she went missing; classes began on August twenty-first. Her home is in McDonald. She has an older sister, Christie, twenty-two, also at UT, a senior. They were roommates. Their father is dead. Their mother remarried and is living in Florida.

"I don't know about the connection yet, Kate," I said. "It's tenuous at best—we have three college students all strangled and found on the north end of the city, or thereabouts. That's it."

She looked at me, her head cocked to one side. It was a look I knew well, and it meant an argument was coming.

"Before you start in on me," I said, "let me go through the files on the other two girls and see what I can come up with, if anything. Okay?"

She looked hard at me, then nodded slowly.

"Good," I said, and then Kate's phone rang.

She flipped the lock screen, listened, then said, "We'll be there in five."

I got to my feet. "Time to go?"

"Yeah. They'll be at the Forensic Center in ten minutes."

Chapter 6

Sarah Foote and the sister arrived just a couple of minutes after Kate and I did. The girl was, I imagined, almost a clone of the one I'd seen opened up on Doc's table: five-seven, a hundred and ten pounds, blonde hair that came from a bottle—the dark roots were showing—and a slim, almost anorexic figure, but a pretty face that I knew could turn heads. And… she'd been crying, and still was, a little. Her eyes were red and puffy and her nose was… well, you get the idea.

Detective Foote made the introductions. Doc Sheddon was conspicuously absent, but that wasn't unusual; Carol Oats performed what would have been his duties with sympathy and respect.

We, including Christie Hart, stood behind the glass partition while Carol gently pulled back just enough of the white sheet to show the girl's face.

For a long moment, Christie Hart stared at the face on the gurney… and then she burst into tears, her hands covering her face, her body shaking with the violence of her sobs.

Me? It's difficult to remember exactly how I felt then. I can only describe it as a deep sense of sadness mingled with almost uncontrollable rage and a driving need to kill something. No, not something. The person or persons who did this terrible thing to this girl, to her sister, and possibly to two more innocent young women. As always, I was struck with wonder as I tried to get into the mind of the killer.

I looked at the face of the girl on the gurney and tried to imagine myself on top of her, my hands around her neck, squeezing; gently at first and then slowly increasing the pressure, looking down into eyes that reflected the terror of what was happening to her; watching as they bulged, soaking in every tremor and jerk of her body as she fought for breath.... *Jesus H. Christ.*

The experts say that to catch a killer you have to be able to think like one, but that's a trite old adage that will get you nowhere. It's easy to say, but almost impossible to do. The average human mind just doesn't work that way. To be able to think like a killer, you have to be one. Ideally you'd be a sociopath: inwardly devious, sly, scheming, ruthless, and inordinately cruel.

As far as I know, I've met only a couple of people who filled that bill in its entirety: Little Billie Harper, now dead, and a woman by the name of Mary Ann Warren. She was all of the above, but underneath a facade of normality. Both were killers—Billie ordered it done; Mary Ann had no problem getting her own hands dirty. She killed coldly and without remorse.

No. I couldn't do it. Hell, I can kill, yeah, but only when I have to, and as a last resort. I believe every life is worth something, especially to its owner, and I can't... I just can't.

And so I listened as Christie Hart formally identified her sister. She nodded and then, when asked, stated verbally for the record that it was indeed Margaret Hart—Maggie—who lay on the gurney, quietly but not at rest. That wouldn't happen until I brought her killer to justice… and I had a deep-seated feeling that she, Maggie, wasn't going to let me rest either.

"Ms. Hart," Kate said as we walked together from the rear door of the Center to the parking lot, "I know this is probably the very worst time to ask, but it can't be helped. We have questions that need answers." The girl turned to look at her. Her cheeks were wet, but she wiped her eyes and nodded.

"Do you feel up to it?" Kate asked. Her voice was so gentle.

Christie shrugged. "Not really, but if…."

"It is. Time is not on our side, and we need to catch whoever did this to Maggie, okay?"

Again, the girl nodded.

"Good. Detective Foote will take you to my office. I'll be there in just a few minutes."

We watched them go, then Kate said, without turning her head, "You up for this, Harry?"

"Oh yeah."

Chapter 7

We arrived back at the Police Services Center at just after twelve thirty that afternoon and headed straight for Kate's office.

Interview rooms are not—how should I put this—designed for comfort. Just the opposite, in fact. They are usually stark places, concrete boxes with bare walls and minimal furniture—usually a sturdy steel table bolted to the floor and three or four chairs. So it was no wonder that Kate had decided to interview Christie Hart in her office instead, although it was barely a notch above the interview rooms comfort-wise.

Christie Hart and Detective Foote were already there, seated and waiting, when Kate and I entered. The only other chair in the room was Kate's, so I stepped out to get one. It wasn't that I needed to sit, but I'm a big guy, and in a small office my size can be intimidating, so I sat, just in front of Christie and to her left at the right side of Kate's desk.

Kate touched the button that started her recorder, then began.

"Ms. Hart. Christie. Just so that we don't miss or forget anything, I'm going to record what we say here. Is that alright?"

Christie nodded.

"I need you to say it out loud, please."

"Yes. It's okay."

"Good. For the record then…." And she went into the standard preamble: the date, time, and location of the interview, all of the individuals present, and the purpose of the interview.

"Now, please tell me about that afternoon, when you last saw Maggie."

And she did, but there was very little to tell. Christie got out of class around three that afternoon, then picked up her sister, and they went to Hamilton Place Mall together, did a little shopping, a little browsing, and then headed back to their apartment on Oak Street. I believed every word she said. I'd been there, done that, so many times… it was just another ordinary day on campus.

"Did you, at any time that afternoon, notice anyone watching you? Following you?"

She shook her head and wiped her eyes, then her nose. "No."

"Did she have plans for that night, other than going for a run?"

"No, I don't think so. She didn't say anything about going out or anything…."

"Okay," Kate said quietly. "So now I want you to think back over the past few weeks. Did she ever mention that she thought she was being watched or followed?

She made the effort, closed her eyes for a moment, then shook her head again and said, "No. Never."

"Have you ever thought that *you* might be being watched or followed?"

Her head snapped up, her eyes wide. "Nooo! No, of course not."

Kate looked at me and nodded.

"Christie," I said gently. "Tell us about her friends. Did she have any boyfriends?"

She shrugged. "She had some friends that were boys, but not boyfriends per se… although… no."

"Although what? Who were you thinking of, Christie?" I asked. "Even if it doesn't seem like it, it could be important."

She shook her head, closed her eyes, and pursed her lips, as if she were trying to deny the thought.

"There is one…. Joey, Joey Lister. He's asked her out a couple of times, but she always said no. The last time was a couple of days before she… before she…." She grabbed a tissue from the box and dabbed her eyes. Then she shrugged and stared at me.

I tapped the name into my iPad. "Were you there?" I asked. "How did he take it when she told him no?"

"I was, yeah. He seemed okay with it. He just smiled at her, and me."

I nodded. "Anyone else? Maybe someone who might be holding a grudge?"

She thought for a moment, then started nodding slowly, her face hardening. "She had a nasty break up with a boyfriend, but that was almost two years ago. Bobby Haskins. They'd been friends since sixth grade. I don't know how serious they were—I know he was, very, but Maggie… I don't think she really was. Anyway, when they graduated high school, she broke it off. He didn't take it well. Followed her for months until Charlie warned him off."

Kate, who had also been making note of the names, asked, "Charlie who?"

"Charlie Elkins. He's two years older than me. Our dad died in a car wreck seven years ago, and Mom, well, she married a real asshole a couple of years later. Charlie… he's nice. Really nice. He kinda took us both under his wing, protected us both."

I nodded. The suspect list was growing.

"This Charlie Elkins…. Did she ever…."

"Go out with him? I think he asked her once, but no. I don't think so."

"That afternoon, up until the time she left the apartment, did she receive any phone calls, texts, messages?"

She had to think about that one. "No… at least not while she was with me. Well, a couple of texts from girlfriends, I think."

"Girlfriends?" I asked, my eyebrows raised.

"Oh no," she said quickly. *Maybe a little too quickly.* "I don't mean like that."

"No, of course not," I said, making a mental note to check it out. "Can you give me their names please?"

"I don't know who texted her, but it might have been Jess Little, her closest friend that I know of. She lives in Cleveland, but she's also a student here. She lives at home with her parents. I can give you her cell number if you like."

I nodded and made a note of it. "What about Maggie's cell phone? We didn't find it. Did she leave it at home?"

"No. She had it with her. She didn't go anywhere without it. She carried it in an arm pocket with her keys."

I looked at Kate. She nodded and picked up her iPhone and sent a text. I could guess what it was about. We needed to ping that phone. If we could find it….

"Christie," I said. "This is important. You said she went to the Riverwalk. Do you know exactly where?"

The Riverwalk runs from Ross's Landing downtown all the way to the Chickamauga Dam, about ten miles end to end. We needed to know where she went and how she got there.

"She would have gone to the dam," she said, "and then run to the Fishing Park and back. It's about a three-mile round trip."

"How did she get to the dam?" I asked. "It's what? Five, six miles from where you live on Oak to the parking lot? She must have driven. What make and model car did she have?"

"A 2013 blue Honda Civic, but it's still in her parking space on campus. She must have gotten a ride, I suppose, but that's not like her. She always drove herself. She liked to be able to come and go as she pleased."

"I'll need the tag number and the address of the parking lot, please, Christie." Kate said.

She gave it to her. Kate buzzed through to Lonnie back in the incident room, and gave him instructions to have the car recovered and taken to forensics.

I looked at Kate and said, "We should get someone over there to check the dorms and rentals to see if anyone saw her getting into a car."

"Sarah," Kate said to Detective Foote, "you can get started on that. See if Tommy Holtz is out there. If he is, take him with you. Canvas that whole area. Knock on doors. If she did catch a ride, there's a good chance someone saw it."

Foote got up and left, and I turned again to Christie Hart.

"So," I said. "Other than you, who were her friends? Who did she hang out with when she wasn't studying?"

"She didn't do that much. She was almost always studying. But she knew lots of people. She was popular. One of the… you know, the in-crowd."

"Was she a member of a sorority?" Kate asked.

"No. She hated those people."

"Oh? Why was that?"

"I don't really know. She… she thought they all were… arrogant, egotistical… I don't know. I just know she had a problem with what she called the 'superior beings.' I suppose that was it. We came from the—well, not exactly the wrong side of the tracks. Just… we weren't rich, I guess."

Believe it or not, I understood what she was trying to say, completely. I confess, I'd never had the problem, and I wouldn't have, because I myself was a member of the privileged class, but I knew plenty of good people who had. Somehow though, I'd managed to stay above—or below, depending upon how you view things—the snobbery that many of Chattanooga's elite wore like a badge of honor. The class system was alive and well in Chattanooga.

"Did she have any close friends, buddies she spent time with?" I asked.

"Jess Little was probably her closest friend, but she also hung out with Jeannie Flowers and Diane

Lane. Like I said, she had a lot of friends, but those three were probably closer to her than any."

I looked at Kate.

"What was her mood, Christie?" Kate asked. "Was she depressed, preoccupied, happy, what?"

"She was *fine*. Happy enough—well, you know, upbeat, I guess. As far as I know she had nothing other than school on her mind. She never said anything."

"What was she like? She was an art major, right?"

"Yes. She was a beautiful person, outgoing, happy, always laughing, friendly, an athlete, a sculptor, gifted…." Tears welled up in her eyes and she began to sob softly.

"Okay," Kate said gently. "I think that's enough for today. I'll have someone drive you home." She turned off the recorder, picked up the phone, and turned in the request.

"It'll be a few minutes. You can wait in the lobby. I'll show you the way…. What about your mother, Christie? She needs to know. Would you like me to have someone in Florida contact her for you?"

She nodded.

"I'll need the address."

She gave it to her along with the phone number.

"I'll call the St. Augustine police department and have them send someone. Is that okay with you?"

Again the nod. *Strange....*

"Do you and you mother get along?" I asked.

She shrugged. "I suppose.... We talk now and then, but it's always all about her, and him, mostly him. It gets old, you know?"

I nodded. "How about Maggie? Did she get along with her mother?"

"I guess. She never talked about her. She didn't like Keith—that's her husband. He's Welsh, a Welshman."

"Why didn't she like him?"

"He's an ass... and Maggie always said he only married Mom for her money. Dad had made some money on the stock market and he was well insured when he died. So.... Well, he's an ass. He doesn't know what the word 'work' means."

There was a knock on the door. It opened, and a uniformed officer stuck her head in. "You asked for a car and driver? I'm the driver." She grinned.

***

Christie Hart went with the "driver" and Kate and I were left alone in her office. Kate leaned back in her chair and stared at me, waiting for me to speak. I looked at my watch, then back at her.

"I hate this place," I said. "I'm beginning to feel like I never left. It's almost three o'clock—you want to grab a bite at the Boathouse?"

She hesitated for a moment, then said, "Yeah. Why not."

The Boathouse is a popular spot just a couple miles from the station, on Riverside Drive. When we're working together we eat there quite often. The excuse? It's easy to get to, the view is amazing, the food is good and so is the beer. At three in the afternoon on a Tuesday it wasn't busy, and we were able to get a table outside with a view overlooking the river and… the Riverwalk.

I ordered a catfish po-boy with fries and a Blue Moon, no orange slice; Kate got a veggie panini, no fries, and an iced tea.

We said little while we waited for our food. When it came, we ate pretty much in silence. It was obvious she had something on her mind.

"Okay," I said, finally. "What's up? What's pissed you off?"

She looked sharply up at me, picked up her glass, sipped, and looked at me over the rim. "Nothing. What makes you think there is?"

"I've known you too long, Kate. I know your moods, so out with it. If we're going to work together, we need to clear the air."

She stared at me coldly. It was a look that I'd seen many times before. It was usually reserved for the bad guys. *What the hell?*

"First, you made me beg; I thought you thought more of me than that. Second, you humiliated me in front of half the PD. You'll never do either one of those things again."

Ah, so that's it. Damn!

I dropped my head, sighed, nodded, then said, "Yeah, I did, didn't I? On both counts." I looked up at her, locked eyes with her. "I'm sorry. It won't happen again. I was… well, I already told you why I didn't…. Look, there's no point in beating it to death. Forgive me?"

She gave me a look of total exasperation, then nodded. "Yeah, of course…." She shook her head. "I guess I have to, don't I." She put her glass down. "What changed your mind, anyway?"

I shrugged. "You know me," I said as I stared out over the river. "Things tend to weigh heavily on my mind, especially… well, I couldn't sleep, and finally, when I did, I dreamed about her…. She spoke to me, Kate. She asked me to help her. It seemed so real." I shrugged again, picked up my glass, and sucked in enough liquid to drown a good-sized horse.

"It was just a dream, Harry. We all have them. They never last."

"No, they never do. Ten minutes after I wake up I can't remember a thing, usually. This time, though, I remembered it all. It was so real. We have to catch this bastard."

"That's a given, Harry. How we do it is something else again. We've never had to deal with anything like this before. It might not be random, but as far as we know it's motiveless. Why does someone do this stuff? Yeah, I know, they're sick, but...."

I had to think about it. I had to return to the lecture hall at Fairleigh Dickenson. I had to think about stuff I hadn't thought about in almost a quarter century. What I learned back then was probably way out of date, but I gave it a try.

"Kate, we don't know for sure yet if these murders are connected."

She glared at me.

"Okay, let's say they *are* connected. If they *are* connected, they are *not* random, and if that's the case, they're not motiveless either."

She leaned forward, placed her elbows on the table, and rested her chin on her knuckles. "How so?"

"Motive," I said. "It's true that serial killers operate differently from regular murderers—if there is such a thing—but they still have motives for what they do. Different ones, yes. Usually murders are about money, revenge, love, hate, jealousy, and so on; you know that."

She nodded.

"Serial killers are almost always sociopaths. They have no feelings of empathy or sympathy. They couldn't care less about their victims. They are, for the most part, devoid of emotions. They don't love or hate, or feel guilt or remorse. They are always pathological liars; you have to be, to keep that kind of thing hidden. And when they kill it's almost always about power, control, sexual gratification. Most of them are extremely charming, persuasive, clever, and manipulative. Remember Ted Bundy? He was the epitome of the type. They rationalize everything they do, so there's never any reason why they should stop. They know right from wrong, and they know the consequences of getting caught, and they know how to avoid getting caught."

"I don't see these killings as random, Harry. I think these girls were chosen, for a reason."

"Yes, you may be right, but they very well could be random. UTC could be the honey pot, the candy store where the killer shops for his victims; it wouldn't be the first time."

"So what kind of person are we talking about?"

I thought for a minute, then said, "There are several types of serial killer. There are the crazies who hear voices that drive them to kill; many of them are convinced they are doing God's will. Then there are those that focus on the act of killing itself; they usually kill quickly and violently and enjoy it so much they become addicted to it. Others focus on the *process* of killing. They kill slowly because they like to prolong the suffering of their victims; it gives them a sense of power. They experiment; they get to decide when and how the victim will die. I think that's what we may be dealing with here… if they are indeed connected."

“Oh they’re connected,” Kate said, gazing out over the water. “I know they are.”

“Maybe,” I said. “I need to study the other two cases. Listen. I have copies of the three murder books. I think maybe I should go to my office and do a little work on them. You might want to come with me. Sound good?”

She looked at her watch. “Harry, it’s already almost four. I can spare an hour.”

“So let’s get out of here.”

I paid the bill, and we left.

***

“So talk to me,” I said, dropping the three binders on my desk. “Tell me about the first one. The one that was found on VW Drive. We know how she died and when, and we know who reported her missing, but there must be more, right?”

“That’s Dana Walters,” Kate replied. “She was reported missing on October eighth almost a year ago. She was a psych major with a minor in criminal justice.”

“She was just strangled to death,” I said.

“We don’t know that. The body was badly decomposed. The neck area was almost totally skeletonized: very little soft tissue remained. The hyoid was fractured so, yes, she was manually strangled, but more than once? We’ll never know.”

I nodded as I stared down at the close-up photograph of the head and neck.

"Was the roommate, Natalie Gibson, able to provide you with anything useful?"

"Depends on what you call useful. We recorded all of the interviews. If Lonnie did as I asked, you should have everything on CDs in the front pockets."

I looked. They were there. "So," I continued, "judging by that answer, what you're telling me then is that your interviews with regard to Dana Walters disappearance and subsequent death have produced nothing we can work with, no suspects. If they had, you'd have told me by now, right?"

She looked uncomfortable. "Yeah, I suppose. Maybe if you go through them…."

"Yeah," I said. "I'll do that. And I suppose it's the same story with regard to the second girl, Jasmine Payne?" I closed one file and opened the second, then looked up Kate.

She shrugged. "Basically it's the same story. She went out around eight on the evening of Monday July tenth. She was supposed to meet friends at Starbucks, but she never arrived. Her roommate reported her missing the following morning."

"What time was that?"

"The call was timed in at 8:07. They had separate rooms. When Jasmine didn't show up ready to go to class the roommate, Amy Lewis, opened the door and found the bed hadn't been slept in. She contacted one the friends Jasmine was supposed to have met the night before, found out she didn't show, and then called 911."

"You talked to the friends, right?"

She gave me a withering look. "What do you think, Harry?"

I nodded. "So nothing worth repeating, then?"

"I don't know," she said, exasperated. "Listen to the damn interviews. Maybe you'll catch something I missed. I got a couple of names out of the interviews and that's it, other than that she wasn't depressed, suicidal.... Oh for God's sake, Harry. If there'd been anything solid, I would have run it down."

"You said you'd gotten a couple of names?"

"Yeah, two boys she'd dated a few times. I talked to both of them. They knew nothing. They hadn't been invited to Starbucks. Neither of them had seen her in a couple of days or more. They were dead ends."

"Did either of them know Dana Walters?"

"No, at least they said they didn't."

"How about her, Dana? Did any of her friends know Jasmine?"

"No."

I flipped open Dana's file and set it alongside Jasmine's. Then I did the same with Maggie Hart's slim file. There they lay, staring up at me. Again, as

I looked down Maggie's face, the dream came flooding back: the wide staring eyes, the raspy voice.... I flipped the file closed and shook my head to rid myself of the image.

"What?" Kate asked. "What is it?"

"Nothing, just a flashback is all. Nothing worth talking about."

She glanced at her watch. "Harry, I hate to run, but I do have an appointment."

"Okay," I said, closing the files. "I'll take these home and listen to the interviews there. I'll meet you in the incident room at eight thirty tomorrow morning, that sound good?"

She nodded.

"I'll need a pass. Will you leave one at the desk for me?"

She said that she would, and then I headed out.

***

Before I left the office that evening, I had a visit from my two new partners.

Jacque was carrying two cups of coffee; one for her and one for me, I hoped. Bob carried his usual pint mug.

I smiled up at them both over the top of the pile of files on my desk.

"Jacque," I said, grabbing the proffered cup, "you are a lifesaver."

I clasped the sides of the cup in both hands, put my elbows on the desk, closed my eyes, and breathed in the heady aroma of Dark Italian Roast—and suddenly the world didn't seem quite so bleak.

"Siddown," I said. "Take a load off. I hope your day was better than mine." They sat, and I sipped; they sipped, and then Jacque spoke, "We bin tinking, Bob an' me." She was obviously a little nervous.

Oh hell, that accent is not a good sign.

I stared over the rim of the cup at her, then at Bob. "Well? Go on."

"We've been thinking—" the accent was gone "—and talking. What you did to us this morning, the bombshell you dropped on us, and then left us swinging in the wind like that; it took a little swallowing, and so did the consequences."

"Consequences?" I asked. "What consequences? You get a piece of the action and I get to take it easy in return. It's as simple as that."

"Simple to you, maybe," Bob grunted over the top of his mug, "but we, well me anyway, haven't run anything in our lives." He looked at Jacque. She nodded.

"Harry. This is a major business," he continued. "There are sixteen employees and a dozen more sub-contractors, and according to Jacque, we're billing more that eleven million a year."

"So what are you saying? You want more money?"

"No, no, nothing like that, but it's a big responsibility and we…." He trailed off, obviously unable to articulate his concerns.

I looked at Jacque. She looked down at her hands.

"So if it's not about the money, what the hell is it?"

"Damn it, Harry," Bob growled. "I'm not sure I'm up to it."

I know my mouth dropped open. The guy had one of the sharpest brains I'd ever come across. I never could understand why the hell he was satisfied working for me. I looked at Jacque. She shrugged… and then it hit me.

"You're worried I'm not going to do my bit," I said. "That I'll leave you to sink. What the hell's the matter with you both? I have almost ten years invested in this company. If that's the way I wanted it, I would have sold the company. I didn't. I turned to you two. I figured that *between us*, we could move onward and upward and share the hard times and the good."

I glared at them. "Look, I'll carry my end of the load. Money is not a problem. I can keep this thing afloat for years if I have to, but I won't have to. I'm back, and I now have an asset I never had before, namely you two. Are we good?"

They looked at each other. Bob grinned at Jacque, she smiled back at him, and then they turned to me and told me we were.

"Good," I said. "Now. How about the clients? How's that going?"

"That was the major part of our concerns," Jacque said. "Bob and I have been making calls all day, making promises we weren't sure we could keep. Now we know we can. We've contacted about a fourth of them. For the most part, they're on board. One or two want a personal reassurance from you. Once we've called everyone, I'll have list for you. You can either call them yourself or visit them, depending on how you rate them."

"They're all important," I said. "If the list isn't too long, I'll hit the trail, talk to all of them. If not… well, I'll figure that out when the time comes." I looked at my watch. It was almost five thirty. I was running late… not for anything important. I just wanted to get out of there and go home.

"Look," I said seriously. "I understand your concerns. Push them away. You have a job to do, and so do I. You do yours as you see fit, and I'll help all I can within the bounds of the commitment I've made to Kate and Chief Johnston. If you need me, I'll be no more than a phone call away. Can you work with that?"

They looked at each other, then looked back at me and nodded.

"Good. Now, unless there's something else, I need to leave." I started to get to my feet.

Jacque sighed. "We'll talk again soon." She stood, turned to Bob, and said, "Let's go."

I watched them close the door behind them, not sure if I was doing the right thing, throwing them in at the deep end like that. But what the hell. I needed my own autonomy. I gathered up the three murder books and headed for the door. *They either make it work, or....*

Chapter 8

Amanda was already home when I got there. In fact she was in the pool, swimming slow laps. I dropped the three files on my desk—I have an office in the basement; Amanda calls it my man cave, but it's not—and went to the kitchen and poured a gin and tonic that would have drowned a large dog for myself, and a much smaller one for Amanda. Then I went out to join her.

I seated myself at the table under the umbrella and sat down to watch her. She is, let me tell, easy to look at, especially when she's wearing that pink bikini.

Eventually she turned and swam over to me, leaned her arms on the edge, cocked her head to one side and squinted in the rays of the evening sun.

"Gimme," she said, stretching out a hand toward me.

I grinned and handed her the drink. She took a single, tiny sip and set it aside. "C'mon, Harry. Get out of those clothes and join me. It's gorgeous in here."

"Nah, I'm too tired to go get changed."

"You don't have to get changed, just strip and jump in. I won't look," she said, a sly smile turning up the corners of her mouth. "Well, maybe a peek."

The look on her face told me she had other things on her mind than just swimming, and that did embarrassing things to me. Nevertheless, I was up for it… yeah, that too. So I turned my back to her and did as she asked. Normally, had I been wearing a swimsuit, I would have dived in. As it was I walked crabwise, both hands strategically placed, to the edge of the pool and hopped in.

"Spoilsport," she whispered as she nibbled my ear.

I love making love in deep water. It's a combination of attempted suicide by drowning and exotic sex that always leaves me choking and gasping for breath; Amanda never has a problem with it. I don't know if it's that she's a better swimmer than me—which she is—or that she simply uses me as a flotation device. Whatever. It's the perfect end to any day—perfect or not.

Ten minutes later we were at the infinity wall together. It was just after eight, and although it was still pretty bright out, the city below was lighting up. I don't know how many hours Amanda and I had spent at the wall since moving into the house over a year ago, but it was a lot.

Anyway, it was quiet up there. The birds had almost quit singing for the night and all I could hear was the soft buzzing of insects. The darkening sky was a riot of red, gold, and orange. Life, as they say, was good, and for the first time in more than two months I felt at peace.

I dropped my hand into the water, let it slide over her bare backside and then up to her waist, and pulled her in close. She nuzzled my neck, sighed, and slipped her arm around my waist.

"You're in a good mood," she whispered in my ear.

"What's not to be in a good mood about?" I asked. "You almost murdered me just a minute ago."

"But you liked it." She bit at my ear.

"Ouch. Quit that. It hurts."

"Oooh, poor baby." She bit me again.

"That's it." I grabbed her waist with both hands and dragged her off the wall and pushed her down under the water. She come up gasping, spluttering and laughing at the same time.

"You pig," she yelled, wrapping her arms around my neck, and down we went. And then she was kissing me, underwater, legs wrapped around my waist, arms around my neck, lips pressed to mine, and slowly we sank to the bottom of the pool. It seemed like an eternity before she let me go and we swam for the surface and the infinity wall.

"I love you, Harry," she said without looking at me. It sounded a little wistful.

"I love you too…. You okay?"

"Better than that. We're going to have a baby." The words tumbled out, and she glanced quickly sideways to look at me.

I was… stunned. Speechless. I'm pretty sure there was a stupid, lopsided grin on my face. "No shit?"

She nodded, slowly. "Harry?"

"Yeah…. Yeah, yeah…. That's… amazing. *Wow,* I'm going to be a *dad.*"

I stared at her. Her eyes were watering and she was smiling. I looked down at her belly. She was up to her shoulders in water. I couldn't see.

"Not yet, silly," she said. "I'm only five weeks along."

"That's, that's… that's…." My head was so full I couldn't do the numbers. "When, for God's sake?"

She laughed. "The last week in April."

"The last week in April," I whispered, almost to myself.

Needless to say, I didn't get any work done that evening. I didn't so much as open the three books. In fact it was well after dark when we finally went into the house, and suddenly I realized I was not only wildly happy, but also ravenously hungry.

We ate scrambled eggs together, and I sipped a glass of cabernet. Amanda drank orange juice. That single, tiny, poolside sip of gin and tonic was the last alcohol she would drink for next eight months. Finally, sometime around midnight, we went to bed. But the evening wasn't quite over, and it was a good thirty minutes later that I finally let go of her, happy, contented, and a somewhat different person.

That night, the dream came again, only this time it was a little different: all three girls, pale, deathly pale, each one talking over the other, the words frantic and garbled so that I couldn't understand what any of them were saying. I woke sweating at four thirty, and sat up in bed. All was quiet. I looked down at Amanda. She was breathing softly, the covers clamped in both hands under her chin. I smiled down at her, then headed for the shower. There would be no more sleep for me that night.

Chapter 9

The shower woke me up. I headed out along Brow Road in the darkness, running hard for the first mile, then I slowed it down to a fast trot and kept heading south, all the way to Covenant College, where I made the turn and headed home. It was just after six when I got back. I looked in on Amanda. She was still sleeping, though the covers were thrown back and she was spread-eagled across the bed, naked. If ever there was a moment to take advantage, that was it. I didn't. Instead I covered her, took another shower, and made coffee.

"Hey," I said, as I placed her cup on the nightstand beside her.

She opened one eye, looked up at me, stretched like a great tawny cat, then sat up and presented me with a pose and a look that meant only one thing.

"Hey lover," she said. "I'm hungry." Now you and I both know what I was thinking that meant, but somehow it never happened. Whether it was the aroma of the coffee or not, I don't know, but she grabbed the cup and started in on it. Then she headed for the bathroom, and she was gone a long time.

In the meantime I got dressed for work: white golf shirt, tan pants, loafers. I slipped my little Glock 43 into its custom-made holster—a Ritchie Leonard special—and headed for the kitchen. The VP9 I'd left in the safe in my office.

More scrambled eggs, two slices of semi-burned toast, and two more cups of coffee, and I was ready for the day.

Well, not quite.

Amanda had joined me for breakfast, but the news she'd dropped on me the night before had so far gone unmentioned.

Finally she looked at me over the rim of her cup, through her eyelashes, and said, "Harry. Are you okay with… well, with the baby?"

"What?" I asked. "Are you serious? I am… *ecstatic*. I never thought it would happen. I'm almost forty-seven, for Christ's sake. Of course I'm okay with it. I'm… I'm… happy as a pig in…. Yeah. I'm happy."

"Me too."

I got up. Went around behind her, slid my hands around her waist, and nuzzled her ear. She giggled.

"Look. I have to go. I didn't get a chance to look through these files last night, so I need to go into the office early and go through them really quick. It's the least I can do before I meet Kate. You okay with that?"

She pouted, but nodded, and I gathered up my stuff, said goodbye, and left her sitting at the breakfast bar nursing her coffee.

It wasn't until I was halfway down the mountain that it really hit me. This was serious stuff. I was going to be a dad! Suddenly I was awash in a tidal wave of weird feelings. I hit the Bluetooth and called Amanda.

"Hey," I said when she picked up. "It just hit me. I mean, really hit me."

She started laughing. "You have no idea how I felt when I walked out of the doctor's office yesterday. I was in a daze. I lost my damned car in the parking lot and had to hit the panic button. Oh Harry, are you happy? Really happy?"

"More than I can tell you. Look, you'd better call Rose or August and have them come over tonight. This kind of news won't keep."

"Are you going to tell them at work? Are you going to tell Kate?"

"Not until we've told August and Rose, and I want to do that with you. Then I'll tell the world."

"Fine. I'll call Rose and tell her that we'll expect them at seven. Don't be late, Harry."

***

I arrived at my offices a little before seven thirty expecting to be first in the door. I wasn't. Both Jacque and Bob had beaten me to it.

"Hey," I said, trying to look as if everything were normal.

"You look strange," Bob said.

"Strange? What do you mean?"

"I dunno. You have a good night last night or something?"

Or something! Hah, you have no idea. "Yeah, I had a good night. A very good night. How about you two?"

"Eh, same as always," Bob said.

Jacque said nothing. She just stared at me, a slight smirk on her face.

"What?"

"Nutin', Boss. Just that you be lookin' good. Coffee?"

"Yeah, coffee, but I can't stay long. I need to meet Kate at eight thirty."

"You want to tell us about what you're doing?" Bob asked.

I didn't. I didn't really have time, but then I figured they had a right to know, now that they were my partners. I set the three murder books down and looked guiltily at them. Yet again, they would have to wait.

By the time I'd finished telling them about the case I was working on it was well after eight o'clock. I had to get out of there. I stood, picked up the three files, and made to leave.

"So why don't you tell us what's really going on?" Jacque asked.

"What? What are you talking about?"

"Come on, Harry," Bob said. "We know you better than you know yourself. There's something you're not telling us. What is it?"

"Nothing. There's nothing. Really."

"How's Amanda?" Jacque asked with a sly smile.

That did it. "She's fine," I snapped, and walked out of my office, leaving them staring after me.

I arrived at the Police Services Center on Amnicola just before eight thirty and, true to her word, Kate had arranged for a visitor's pass. It was waiting for me at the front desk.

I found Kate in her office. Lonnie was sprawled in a chair in front of her desk. I entered, and he pulled his feet out of my way and grinned up at me.

"Right on time. My oh my."

"What's with everyone today?" I growled as I stepped around his chair.

Kate raised an eyebrow. "A little touchy this morning, aren't we?"

"You too? Gimme a break, both of you. Okay?"

They were right, though. For some reason I couldn't put my finger on, I was more than a little antsy. Amanda's status? Maybe. Or maybe it was just the fact that I hadn't taken the time to go through the case files? Whatever. I needed more coffee. I dumped the files on the corner of Kate's desk and went to get some.

That done, I took the empty seat to Lonnie's right and sucked on the steaming liquid that passed for coffee. It was wet and strong, and that was about all. Still…. Finally, I was ready for them.

"Are you with us now?" Kate asked sarcastically.

"Go," I said.

"So you went through the files—what were your thoughts?"

I heaved a huge sigh, shook my head, and said, "No, I didn't. I…. kind of got sidetracked and wasn't able to get to them. Sorry."

She looked at me as if I'd just spit in her eye.

"You didn't look at them at all?" She was incredulous.

I just shook my head.

"Well that sucks." She sat for a moment, staring at me, then said, "You want to take a couple of hours and at least read them through?"

"Later. Right now I'd like to concentrate on the latest case. What do we have? Anything?"

"We're waiting for Foote and Holtz. They're usually here by now." She looked at her watch. "They should have been here ten minutes ago. Damn. Anyway. Let's wait and see what they've found, if anything, and then we'll go see Charlie Elkins. I'd go right now, but I'm waiting for the results of his background check." She paused to check her iPad, then continued, "And Joel Lister's and Robert Haskins's."

I nodded. They would make a good beginning.

"Kate," I said, "if these three killings are connected, we need to figure out what the connection is. Maybe it's UTC, but we need something more specific than that. It's a big campus with more than eleven thousand students and at least a couple of hundred faculty and staff.

"I didn't have time to go through the files yet—sorry—but I know you both have. Is there anything other than the fact that they were all enrolled at the school that grabbed your attention?"

I looked at Kate then at Lonnie. Both shook their heads.

"Dana Walters," Kate said, somewhat absorbed, "and Jasmine Payne were both psych majors, a year apart; Maggie Hart was an art major. So no link there."

"Yeah," I said thoughtfully. "There are plenty of psych majors at UT. It seems to be the flavor of the month. Any idea who the professors were?"

"No. Not yet." She paused. "Harry, I landed the Jasmine Payne case the day she was discovered. I visited the scene while the body was still onsite, and I attended the post. There was nothing. No trace evidence, no DNA. The dump site was clean and so was the body. We did a door-to-door at UTC, but came up empty. Dana Walters.... I dunno yet. I haven't had time to go through that file in depth, but I will, and I know you will. Right now I'm concerned about the timeline for this latest case. The first forty-eight are already gone, and we need to move quickly before we have another cold case on our hands."

She was right. The first forty-eight hours in a murder investigation, in any investigation, are crucial. In this case, however, the girl had already been dead for more than three days when they found her and that was more than forty-eight hours ago. So we were already five days in the hole. We needed to get moving.

The door opened and a uniformed officer stuck her head in. She was holding some papers. "Lieutenant, these are for you. Four sets. I made extra copies. If you need more just give me a buzz."

She dropped them on the desk and left. Kate picked them up, glanced at the top sheet, then handed some to Lonnie and another set to me: a half-dozen sheets of paper stapled together. They were the background checks she'd been waiting for.

We sat together for several moments scanning the reports. I looked up her. She was smiling. So was Lonnie.

"Son of a bitch," Lonnie said. "Elkins is a registered sex offender."

I shook my head. "Don't go there. Not yet. We need to know more."

"Yeah, we do," Kate said, rising to her feet, "and we need to know now. Let's go—ah." Something had caught her eye through the window into the incident room. "Here they are now." She went to the door, opened it, and yelled, "Sarah, Tommy, get in here!

“Where the hell have you two been?” she asked as they entered the office. “It’s almost nine o’clock. No, never mind. I don’t have time to hear it. How did it go on campus? Anything?”

“Not a whole lot,” Holtz said, undaunted by her obvious irritation. “We did a door-to-door of the dorms and apartments, and the sorority houses, talked to a lot of people. She had friends alright, plenty of them. She went for a run almost every evening around six. It was a ritual. Run, shower, dinner, study, bed. No one noticed anything unusual that evening, except for….” He looked at his iPad. “Yeah, one Lacy Morgan—she lives in the dorms.” He flipped through the screens on his iPad. “Block six. She said she thinks she saw our vic get into a light-colored pickup at the corner of Oak and Palmetto. The vic’s Honda would have been parked in the Palmetto lot just three blocks away, so she was probably on her way there. Ms. Morgan says she didn’t take a lot of notice, but thought the vehicle—the one the vic got into—was an older model truck. She thought it might have been a Ford, or a Toyota or something. She couldn’t be sure. Hell, she wasn’t even sure of the day, but she did know it was Maggie Hart and she did remember what she was wearing: red shorts and a black top, so it fits.”

“Did she get a look at the driver?” I asked.

“No. The windows were tinted, but she did say that Maggie was smiling, so she must have known whoever it was, right?”

"Maybe," I said. "But that truck's important. We need to find it, find out if it's owned by someone living or working on campus.... You say she was smiling at the driver, like she knew him, right?"

"That's what the girl said," Holtz replied.

"If she did know him—hell, it could have been a woman driving." I shook my head. "Whatever, it might have been a girlfriend, a boyfriend—" I looked meaningfully at Kate "—or just someone she knew. Either way, the timing is right, so it could have been her killer. If it wasn't her killer, it was probably the last person to see her alive. We need to find that truck."

I turned to Lonnie. "Can we have someone grab some images of pickup trucks from the Internet, say for years between... I dunno, 1970 and 1990?"

"Sarah?" Lonnie looked at her with his eyebrows raised.

She nodded. "I'll get right on it."

"Okay," I said, then paused and turned to Kate. "Look. This is awkward. I can't go around giving orders like I work here. I'm just a visitor...."

"As far as this case is concerned," she said, "you have the chief's blessing, so go ahead and tell 'em what you want. If you have to go through me or Lonnie every time we'll never get anything done. Go for it." She looked at Holtz and Foote. "You hear?"

They both nodded, and so did I.

"Okay," I said to the two detectives. "Lonnie, here's what you do. Download the images to your tablets and then the three of you go back to campus and show them to your witness. See if she can ID the make and model. If she can, Lonnie, you get onto the DMV and try to track it down. If not, you split up and hit every dorm, apartment building, and sorority and frat house on campus. Hit the dining halls, rec areas, study halls, libraries. Show the images to anyone who'll take a look. I don't care how long it takes. That truck is the only real lead we have. We need to find it. Yeah?"

They all nodded.

"Okay. Get to it. If you find anything, call Lieutenant Gazzara immediately; call me if she doesn't answer. If not, be back here before five for a progress report. Make a note of my number."

They did, and then they left.

"Well," I said to Kate, "it's something."

She nodded, but her mind was obviously on other things. "Let's go see Mr. Elkins," she said.

Mr. Elkins would be one Charlie Elkins, Maggie Hart's so-called guardian angel. He lived in a small rental house on East Fifth Street. From the outside it was a clean little home, not exactly on the UTC campus, but near enough not to make much difference. With Kate at my side, I thumbed the doorbell and we waited.

"Mr. Elkins?" Kate asked, holding out her badge for him to see when he opened the door.

He was tall but not handsome—ugly, even. The sides of his head were shaved all the way above his ears, leaving a shock of spiky, bottle-blond hair on top. He was slim but muscular, and he was dressed in baggy shorts that came below his knees and a white T-shirt with the arms cut off. He sported intricate tattoos of snakes entwined around both shoulders, which was probably the reason for the missing sleeves. He was also wearing glasses, thick, Coke bottle glasses. He leaned forward, squinted at the badge, then at me, then at Kate.

"Yeah, you're police alright," he said. "What do you want? Is this about Maggie?"

"My name is Lieutenant Catherine Gazzara. This is Detective Harry Starke," she replied.

Wow, I'm a detective again?

"I understand," she said, "that you were a friend of Maggie's."

He nodded. "I was. I can't believe…. I can't believe she's gone. She was so… she was a lovely person."

"Can we come in for a few minutes, Mr. Elkins? We have a few questions, if you don't mind."

He stood back and opened the door wider so we could get past him. The foyer on the other side was tiny, but Kate and I crowded into it while he closed the door.

"This way," he said, and he led us into what I assumed was the living room.

The room contained little furniture other than a sectional couch, none too clean, a sixty-inch flat screen TV, and a large coffee table.

"How about we go to kitchen or dining room?" I nodded at the couch. "That thing is too low for me."

"Sure, the kitchen is fine."

We sat around the table. Kate and me on one side, Elkins on the other. This guy didn't believe in doing the dishes. They were stacked high on the counter, and the sink was full. An open pizza box with a single slice left in it was open on the table, along with five empty Bud cans.

"What can I do to help?" he asked.

I looked at Kate. She nodded.

I needed to make friends with him, so that was what I tried to do. "Thank you for agreeing to talk to us," I said sincerely, looking him directly in the eyes. "You knew Maggie and her sister well, I'm told. You were *good* friends with her?"

He shrugged. "Good? Yeah, I suppose."

"Yes, Christie, her sister, mentioned that you were. How about Maggie's other friends?" I asked. "Did she have a lot?"

"She did. She was pretty popular."

"Anybody in particular?" I asked.

"Well, Jessica, I suppose. And a few others, but Jessica was her best friend, I think."

"That would be Jess Little?" I asked.

"Yeah. Her."

"And the others?"

"Jeanie Flowers, Diane Lane… Ruthie, Ruth Morton, I suppose."

"How about Joey Lister?"

"Hah! He should be so lucky. In another lifetime, maybe. Who told you that?"

"No one," I said. "Christie mentioned she thought he'd asked her out. Do you know if he did?"

"Oh yeah. The little creep. He was always asking her out, but she'd have none of it. She didn't have *any* boyfriends. Not that I know of."

"How about you, Charlie?" Kate asked, quietly. "Did you ever take her out?"

He looked away, shook his head. A little too quickly. "No. She wasn't my type." *Hmmm. Christie said you asked her out at least once. What's that about?*

"So tell me about Joey," I said. "Was he a nuisance, a stalker, what?"

He thought for a minute, then shrugged. "He's a creep. Not even worth calling a nuisance."

"You don't like him," Kate said. "Why not?"

"What's to like? He's one of those little people who's there every time you look around, somewhere, watching… creepy little bastard."

"A stalker, then?" Kate asked.

He slowly shook his head. "Nah, not really. Just a wannabe. You know? A suck up. Maggie was nice enough to him, but I kicked his ass a couple of times—well, once. Told him not to bother her, but he didn't seem to get it."

"Christie said you… well, that you looked after her and Maggie, so to speak," Kate said.

"Looked after her… no, not really. She was pretty independent. She could look after herself."

"But Christie told us that you warned off Maggie's old boyfriend." She glanced down at her iPad. "Robert Haskins. Bobby."

"I did more than warn him off. I beat the shit out of him. Now *there's* your stalker. Maggie dumped him and he wouldn't have it, couldn't accept it. He followed her around. Sat outside her dorm half the night watching her window. Texting her at all hours. Phoning, hanging up when she answered, texting her if she didn't. Then one day he put his hands on her, bruised her arm and, well…. I figured it had gone far enough, and I put a stop to it, as far as I know…. Oh shit! You don't think…?"

"No. We don't," Kate said. "Christie didn't tell us you'd had a violent confrontation with Haskins. She just said you'd warned him off."

"Well she's right, I did. Couple of times, but he didn't get the message. I found him sitting outside her dorm one night and I dragged him out of his truck and… well, after that he quit. At least, Maggie said he did."

Kate and I looked at each other. "You dragged him out of his truck," she asked. "What sort of truck was it?"

"I dunno. An old Ford, I think. I never paid much attention to it. Not the sort of ride I'd be seen dead in. Some piece o' shit junker."

Kate looked at me. I nodded.

"What kind of vehicle do you drive, Charlie?" she asked.

"A 1985 Ford Bronco, full size."

"What color?"

"Blue and white."

She nodded and made a note of what he'd said on her iPad. "Let's talk for a minute about Maggie. What was she like?"

"Very pretty. Not sexy, like, but hot…."

"That's not what I meant," Kate said a bit sharply. "What sort of person was she?"

"Oh. Well, she was nice, quiet… worked hard, I guess. Studied a lot. I dunno. She was… a nice person."

"Okay, Mr. Elkins," Kate said, getting up from the table. "That, I think, will be enough for today. If we need to talk to you again, I'll let you know."

We rose from the table and headed for the door. I followed Kate. Then I turned again. "By the way, Charlie, where were you that afternoon, August the thirtieth, between… say, five thirty and seven?"

He looked kinda put out, but answered quickly enough. "I was here. All evening. Why?"

"Just a thought," I said. "Anyone with you?"

"No. I was just watching TV. Is there something…?"

"No, no. I had to ask. It's what we do. Have a good day, Mr. Elkins." And then I did it again. Talk about Colombo. "Mr. Elkins, does the name Jasmine Payne ring a bell?" *Did his eyelids just flicker?*

"No. Should it?"

"No, just asking. How about Dana Walters?"

He shook his head. I nodded and closed the door behind me.

"You didn't bring up his background," I said when we were back inside the unmarked cruiser.

"No, I thought you were going to," Kate said. "You didn't, so I figured you had something else in mind, that you were saving it for another day, and if so, you were right to. He can't escape his past. There's time for that later. Right now he doesn't know we know, and he's talking to us, and that's good. We'll need to talk to him again, but in the proper environment. By the way, did you believe him?"

"About Maggie not being his type? No. I'd believe Christie before I'd believe him and, from what I've seen of her photographs, she was quite beautiful; he'd have to be a damned zombie not to have at least tried, and a zombie he isn't. He protected her from Haskins, beat the crap out of him, so he said, and from Joey Lister, so he must have thought something of her, right?"

"Yeah…." She shook her head. "So now we need to talk to Haskins—Robert, Bobby, whatever. And we need to take a look at his truck."

I nodded. "So let's go."

Chapter 10

Robert Haskins lived with his mother on Brently Wood Drive, just off East Brainerd Road. They'd moved there from Cleveland in 2015 so that she wouldn't have to travel so far to get to work; she was an inspector at the Volkswagen plant. Kate drove, so I was able check his background report on the way to his home. He was twenty-one, graduated from Bradley High School in 2014 and was, judging by his grades, no great genius. His credit score was in the mid-five hundreds, which meant he had no credit. But he had no criminal history either, not even a parking ticket. He'd gone to work for Jesper Construction when he left school and had stayed there. Not the worst report I'd ever read.

He wasn't home when we got there. His mother answered the door and told us he was at work, which he was. He was working on a major project, an addition to Erlanger Hospital. Fortunately, it was lunchtime when we arrived and we found him sitting with a group of coworkers in one of the ground-floor rooms.

We asked him if he wouldn't mind giving us a few a minutes to answer some questions. He looked a little wary, but he packed up his lunch and we went outside and sat down on one of those benches donated by grateful patients, or their families.

Haskins was one of those kids you'd never notice until he did something that grabbed your attention. He was maybe five foot ten with close-cropped black hair, clean shaven, muscular as most construction workers are, and deeply tanned, so deeply tanned that the tattoos on both arms were difficult to make out, though one did catch my attention. On his left shoulder, as close to my face as I felt comfortable to get, was a large red rose with the name Maggie written below it in stylized script. On his left forearm was what looked like a scorpion. He was wearing cargo shorts that had seen much better days and a black T-shirt with the words CHECK IT OUT emblazoned in large letters across the front.

Check what out? I wondered.

Kate and I sat him down between the two of us. Not the greatest layout to conduct an interview in, but it was the best we could do under the circumstances.

"Robert," Kate said, leaning forward, her elbows on her knees, "We're here to talk to you about Margaret Hart. You knew her pretty well, right?"

He nodded, looked sad, said, "Yes. I knew her."

I also leaned forward, my elbows on my knees, hands clasped together, "Pretty well?" I repeated, and I watched his eyes.

Again, he nodded—a little reluctantly, I thought.

I looked at Kate. She shrugged. I decided to shake his tree a little, see if anything broke loose.

"Let's not screw around, Bobby. That's what they call you, isn't it? You knew her very well. You knew her since sixth grade, for Christ's sake. You were her boyfriend, until she dumped you."

He reared back on the bench, shocked, his body thudding hard against the backrest.

"I… yes, we dated, but it wasn't serious…."

"Not serious my ass," I said. "You dated her for what, five, six years? You've got her name tattooed on your shoulder for Christ's sake. Don't tell me it wasn't serious."

"Well… okay, so we dated, for a long time. We were both getting bored with it, so—"

"Don't bullshit me, Bobby," I said. "*She* might have been getting bored with it, but you weren't. You took it hard. You stalked her. Where were you the afternoon of August 30, between five and seven o'clock?"

"Whaaat?" He almost screeched it. "What are you trying to say? That I killed her? You're friggin' crazy."

"Where were you, Bobby?" Kate asked quietly.

Way to go, Kate.

"I *dunno*!" He was angry. "I dunno where I was. I can't remember. That was a… what day was it?"

"It was a Wednesday, Bobby," Kate almost whispered. "Surely you remember where you were. It was only a week ago."

Her quiet tone calmed him down some, and he thought for a minute, then said, “I was at work until four thirty, then I went home, showered, and went out to get something to eat. I went to… Zaxby’s on East Brainerd Road. I go there kind of a lot. Mom doesn’t like to cook now that Dad’s gone, so….”

“What time would that have been?” she asked.

“I dunno, five thirty or six, sometime around then. I don’t remember.”

“Did anyone see you there?” she asked.

“I’m sure they did. The place is usually crowded then.”

“Did you eat in or get your order to go?”

“In… no, to go—no, I ate in. I remember.”

“Hmmm,” Kate said. “So you got to Zaxby’s when?”

“I told you. Sixish, I think.”

“Did you have anyone with you that can corroborate your story?” I asked.

He jerked around to look at me. “No,” he said, his eyes squinted in outrage.

“Because you see,” I said, even more quietly than Kate, “Maggie was seen getting into a vehicle at around six o’clock that Wednesday afternoon. Zaxby’s is what, five minutes from the corner of Oak and Palmetto?”

He jumped to his feet. “You’re friggin’ nuts! You are! You think I killed her!” He was almost in tears.

"I wouldn't—I couldn't do that. I loved her. I'll always love her. She was my soulmate."

"Sit down, Bobby," I said, stretching my legs and looking up at him. "We're not done yet."

"But—"

"Sit!"

He sat.

"Tell me about Charlie Elkins," I said.

"What about him?"

"He said, and I quote, 'I beat the shit out of him.'"

He looked sideways at me and, for the first time since we'd met with him, he smiled. "Yeah, that's what he did—in his dreams. The other way around, more like."

"Tell me about it."

"He'd asked Maggie out a few times. She'd turned him down. He was jealous, I guess. I'd just dropped Maggie off at her dorm. He waited till she'd gone in and then he came after me, jerked the truck door open and grabbed my arm. I jumped out, smacked him in the mouth, and down he went. That was enough. He got up and left in a hurry. Easy."

"That's not the way he tells it. He said you hurt her, bruised her arm."

Again the smile. "He said that? Nope. He did that. It was… I dunno, maybe a couple of months ago. She'd just parked her car and was walking back to her dorm. She said he was waiting for her, grabbed her arm. She jerked it free and ran." He shrugged.

"So he wasn't a friend of hers, then?"

"Yeah, but he wanted more. She didn't." Again the shrug. "Look, Maggie and me, we were friends since we were kids, yeah? And we dated for a long time, but then she ended it. I was upset for a while, but I got over it. She was still my friend, and I was hers. I took her out now and again. Nothing to it. No sex, nothin'. That's the truth. That's how it was."

I looked across him at Kate. She shook her head slightly as she looked at me, one of those "I don't know what to believe" looks.

"But you were still in love with her?" Kate asked.

He didn't answer. He just stared down at the floor.

Oh yeah. He loved her.

"What about Joey Lister?" I asked.

He sat up, stared at me, his eyes wide. "Joey? What about him?"

"We understand that he was also interested in Maggie," I said.

"Eh. He's okay. He asked her out a couple of times. She told him no."

"Was he persistent?" Kate asked.

He shrugged. "Did he bother her, you mean? No, not really. She liked him, I think, but not.... Well, you know."

"What do you think of him?" I asked.

What was it Elkins had called him? A creepy little bastard?

Bobby looked sideways at me through narrowed eyes. "He's okay, I guess. Not somebody I'd hang with, but okay."

Kate's phone buzzed. She looked at the screen and then at me. "It's Foote. I'd better take it." She stood and walked far enough away from the bench that she wouldn't be overheard. She had her back to me, and a thought I hadn't had for more than two years came into my head like a lightning bolt.

Wow. Nice ass!

And I knew firsthand just how nice it really was. I shook my head to rid myself of the unwanted intrusion—but her ass really was nice.

"That was Foote," she said, coming back toward us. "It seems Ms. Hart was seen getting into a two-tone, light-colored Chevy or Ford pickup truck, probably a 1972–74 model. You drive a truck, don't you, Bobby? What make, model, and year would that be?"

He gulped, then shook his head. "It's a 1976 Ford F100."

"And what color is it?" she asked gently.

"Light blue and white," he whimpered, "but it wasn't me, I swear it. I loved her. I did, I did… I… did."

"Okay," she said. "We're going to need to take possession of that truck. Where is it?"

He jumped to his feet. "Screw you. You need a friggin' warrant. You're not getting it without one."

"Oh dear, Bobby," I said. "You're right, we do. Kate, why don't you take our friend here down to headquarters for further questioning while I call Judge Strange. I can have a warrant in… well, it might take a while. Say four this afternoon."

"You can't do that," he yelled. "They'll fire me. What will the guys think if you take me in? Please, don't do this."

"Bobby," Kate said. Her voice had steel in it now. "We need to have forensics go over your truck, if only to eliminate it. If what you say is true, you have nothing to worry about, right?"

"But we were still friends, I told you. I took her out, and I gave her rides a bunch of times, just not that night. She's been in the truck." His face was white. "Okay, okay, dammit," he yelled as he reached in his pocket. I jumped to my feet, my hand reaching for the Glock at my waist. Kate was only a split second slower. We were both premature. He pulled a set of keys from the pocket and flung them at Kate.

"Take the damn thing. I didn't kill her. I didn't see her that night. You've got it all wrong."

Kate pulled her phone and called it in. "Willis will be here in twenty minutes," she said. "Where's the truck, Bobby?"

"Around back, with all the others. I'll show you."

And he did.

"So, do you believe him?" Kate asked, as Mike Willis and his assistant pulled away from the job site with Bobby Haskins's pickup on his flatbed.

"I'm not sure," I said thoughtfully. I watched them round the bend—Haskins, having given Willis written permission for him to take and process his truck, and having received a receipt for it in return, had gone back to work. There was no point in pulling him in just yet.

"I'm not optimistic," she said. "Haskins already admitted she rode in the truck from time to time, so even if we find anything that puts her in the vehicle, unless it's her blood, it's just circumstantial. No help at all."

I nodded. She was right.

"He has no alibi for the time she was seen getting into the truck," I said. "You know what Zaxby's is like at that time of day. We have to try though. You might want to put Foote or Holtz on it…. Hmmm, pity we didn't get photo of him."

She smiled, held up her iPhone for me to see, and there he was, looking back at me.

"When did you get that?"

“Hey, you’re not the only smart one. I grabbed it right after Foote called about the truck. I got one of Elkins, too.”

“Not bad, Detective. Not bad at all.”

She forwarded the photo to both Foote and Holtz, then called Foote and gave instructions for them to check Zaxby’s for the night of August thirtieth. It was a long shot, but what the hell. Sometimes long shots pay off.

“Time we talked to some of her friends, I think,” she said as we walked back to her car.

“Yeah, I agree. But before we do, I’d like to complete the picture, talk to suspect number three.” I glanced at my iPad. “Joey Lister. We’ve already got two conflicting stories. It will be interesting to see what he has to say. Then we should probably talk to the so-called BFF, Jessica Little.”

“We should talk to the witness too,” she said.

“Lacy Morgan? Why? What more can she tell us? She didn’t know Maggie. She halfway identified the truck, but she didn’t see the driver…. By the way, did you notice that the windows of Haskins’s truck were tinted? Two-tone truck. 1976 Ford. That’s too many coincidences. I don’t like coincidences. One? Maybe. Two? Doubtful. Three? Not a chance in hell.”

“So you don’t believe him?”

I shrugged. “I’m still trying to figure him out. I was watching him pretty close though, and if he was acting, he’s damned good....”

“Hm. Well.” She turned the key in the ignition. “Let’s go see Joey.”

Chapter 11

Joey Lister was a student at UTC and a member of a fraternity that, for obvious reasons, will remain unnamed. Suffice it to say, it was one of the more minor Greek houses on campus. Unfortunately, he wasn't there. He did spend a lot of time there—so we were told—but he didn't live in the frat house. He actually lived alone in a small rental cottage on O'Neal Street.

"You just missed him," a smarmy-looking individual told us. He made no attempt to hide his admiration for Kate's breasts. Apparently Joey Lister had gone to the Starbucks in the University Center, to meet some friends for coffee. The center was about ten blocks away.

"So," Kate said, "why doesn't he live here at the frat?"

Smarmy ginned at her. It wasn't nice.

He licked his lips salaciously, flapped his tongue at her. "He likes his privacy… if you know what I mean."

She took a step forward, grabbed him by his shirt collar, pulled him in close, and snarled, "Unless you want to waste half a day in an interview room at the police department, you'd better show a little respect, you little piece of shit. Keep your friggin' eyes in your head and your filthy mouth shut. Got it?"

He got it. She shoved him away. He staggered backward a couple steps and then stood looking at her, his mouth hanging open.

Then looked at me, his eyes wide.

"What she said."

"Get out of here," Kate said to him. And he did.

Starbucks, anywhere, is a magnet for students at almost any time of day, so we expected the worst as we drove to the one on campus. We were pleasantly surprised to find the place less than swarming.

But Joey wasn't easy to find. We had no photos of him, so all we could do was split up and canvas the place. Kate found him seated by a window with three girls.

Kate introduced herself, and he agreed to join us for coffee, so we found a quiet place to sit just outside in the lobby: a small, square table with four chairs.

He wasn't at all what I was expecting. Medium height, medium build, smartly dressed in a sky blue golf shirt, tan shorts, and sandals. His light brown hair was neatly trimmed, as was his small mustache. His blue eyes sparkled in the artificial light. He was a good-looking kid.

A creepy little bastard? Not hardly.

"Hey," he said, offering me his hand. "I'm Joey Lister. You are?"

"I'm Harry Starke."

"Whoa, dude. *The* Harry Starke?"

Damn. Here we go.

I sighed, took my hand back, and sat down. "No, just Harry Starke."

"Yeah, but…." He stopped when he saw the look on my face. "Okay, okay, I get it." He looked at Kate, "This is about Maggie, right?"

She nodded. "How well did you know her, Joey? Is it Joe or Joey?"

"Either one. I don't care. Um, I knew her really well. We dated a couple of times. I'd have liked to have known her better, but she was so hung up on her studies…."

"You *dated* her?" Kate asked incredulously.

"Yeah. Not seriously, we only had three dates in maybe four months from… May to August. And we'd see each other for coffee, whatever, one or two times a week, mostly to study together. She was minoring in art history, and I was too…. I can't believe she's gone. What the hell happened to her? Nobody's telling us anything, just that she was found on the Riverwalk."

"Okay," Kate said, obviously still not believing what she was hearing. "You *dated* her, like going on a date-date?"

I couldn't help but smile. Even so, I was finding it hard to swallow myself.

"Yeah, a date. You know," he said, a little sarcastically, "I asked her out. She said yes. We went out. On a date."

"Okay," I said, "enough with the smartass act. Just how well *did* you know her?"

"I told you. I knew her well. Not well *enough*, but we were friends. You know."

"That's not what we heard," I said. "We heard she turned you down, that you stalked her."

"You've been talking to that dickhead Elkins, then. He couldn't even stand me talking to her."

"Did he know you were dating her?" I asked.

"Nah. Not many people did. Maggie wanted to keep it quiet. It wasn't a big deal. I didn't sleep with her or anything. We just went to the movies a couple of times and to dinner. It was nice. She was nice."

"How about Bobby Haskins?" Kate asked. "Do you know him?"

"Nope. Who is he?"

"She never mentioned him to you?"

"Not that I can remember."

"What kind of vehicle do you drive, Joey?"

He looked surprised. "A 2015 Rogue. Why?"

"And where were you on Wednesday August thirtieth between five and seven o'clock?"

"Shit, I don't know." He half closed his eyes, looking somewhat mystified. He thought for a moment, brightened, and continued, "I was at the frat until sometime between five thirty and six, and then at the Bonefish Grill with Jennifer Lockerby. I picked her up from her dorm and we got there around six and left just after seven thirty. You can ask her."

"Don't worry," I said. "We will. Okay, Joey. That's enough for today. You can go now, but we may want to talk to you again."

"Anytime, Mr. Starke. Anytime." He grabbed what was left of his coffee, gave Kate one of those smiles that did little to hide what he was thinking, and then he left and returned to his table and the three girls still seated there.

"Oh, one more thing," I said. He turned.

"Does the name Jasmine Payne mean anything to you?"

"Yeah, of course it does. She was murdered a couple of months ago. Is she… is that connected to…?"

Oh damn. Now it will be all over campus, and the media.

"I can't answer that right now," I interrupted him, trying to gloss over the slip up. "Did you know her?"

"Nope. Not even hardly." There was something about the way he held my gaze.

You son of a bitch. You did *know her.*

I didn't ask him about Dana Walters. I let it go for the moment. I didn't want to hand him any more gossip.

"Quite the ladies' man," I said as I watched him saunter across the room.

"He's a smartass," Kate said. "And you let the damned cat out of the bag."

"Yeah, I did. But we needed to know. He knew Jasmine. I could tell by the look in his eyes. He was almost mocking me. I think he liked you, though," I said, smiling.

The look she gave me that could've frozen a glass of water.

"I get the distinct impression that he likes anything in a skirt," she said dryly. "I think he's one of those guys that lives to exercise his di…. Well, he's a typical arrogant frat boy with a low regard for women. He's privileged and thinks he's entitled to everything. Elkins was right. He *is* a creepy little bastard."

"Wow, Kate. Tell me how you really feel. I didn't get that from him. Smartass, yeah, a little, but…."

She sighed. "You wouldn't, Harry. Sometimes I wonder if you live on the same planet as me, I really do."

"Wow," I said. "That's a first."

"Yeah? You think?"

"You're angry, Kate. Why?"

She lowered her head and shook it. "I just know his type. I ran into one just like him back when I was at UTK. He thought he was God's gift. It didn't end well. I almost broke his arm. Joey Lister reminded me of him."

"Yeah, well. Whatever. But, Kate, you almost broke his arm? Jeez."

"Yes, I did—don't ask. Lister's an open book," she said sourly. "Shallow and affected."

"Shallow? Maybe, but I don't think he was lying, and if his alibi checks out we can eliminate him. What bothers me though is that, if he was dating her, how come no one knew? What was she trying to hide?" I looked at my watch. It was just after two o'clock. "We need to talk to her friends."

"We do," Kate agreed. "And I think we should start with her so-called BFF, Jessica Little."

Chapter 12

Jessica Little lived in Cleveland some twenty-five miles from the UTC campus. Not too far, but….

"I wonder if she's on campus," I said. "It's barely two o'clock; she should be, right?"

Kate shrugged. "Give her a call. We have her number."

So I did. "Jessica? Jessica Little?"

There was silence on the other end of the line. I waited. Then, finally, just as I was about to speak again: "Who is this?" She had a nice, sort of rough-sounding voice, like a lounge singer's.

"My name is Harry Starke. I'm with the police. If you have a few minutes, we'd like to talk to you about Maggie Hart. Are you on campus? Can we meet somewhere?"

The answer came quickly. "Yes, yes of course. I'm sorry. I didn't recognize the number. I almost didn't answer it. I'm at Starbucks, on campus. Will that work?"

I took the phone from my ear. "Damn!" I whispered to Kate. "She here. In Starbucks."

I put the phone back to my ear and said, "That'll be fine. We just left there. We're still outside. There was a table just outside the door—if it's still free, we'll meet you there."

I spotted her walking out of the coffee shop as we were walking toward it.

Kate had her phone to her ear, but she wasn't talking. This time, I knew exactly what she was about to do. As we approached, she lowered the phone and snapped a wide shot of the entrance, making sure to included Jessica. If you didn't know Kate, and Jessica didn't, you'd never know.

She was a natural beauty. Not exactly the stuff of models, but a head-turner nonetheless: five foot eightish, slim, nicely proportioned, blonde hair bobbed just a bit longer than Amanda's and big blue eyes. She was wearing jeans and a white T-shirt with the word CHATTANOOGA emblazoned across the front in big black letters.

"Hi Jessica," I said, offering her my hand. "I'm Harry Starke. This is Lieutenant Catherine Gazzara, with the Chattanooga PD. Thanks for agreeing to talk to us."

"I know who you are, Mr. Starke. Who around here doesn't? But I have to be in class in thirty minutes, so can we make this kind of quick?"

I nodded. "This won't take long. Let's sit, shall we?" We sat. Kate and I took the same seats as we had for our interview with Joey Lister.

"I saw you talking to Joey out here," she said.

"Yes," Kate said. "Do you know him?"

"Unfortunately."

"How so?"

"I made the mistake of going on a date with him. He's a pig."

"Why do you say that?" I asked.

"The bastard tried to rape me. I hit him up the side of the head with this." She pulled a set of keys from the pocket of her jeans. Attached to the ring was what looked like a handcrafted fob: a length of hot pink cord braided onto the ring at one end and what I knew to be a covered, one-inch steel ball at the other. It was, in fact, a Monkey Fist—fourteen feet of military-grade paracord crafted to a final length of about ten inches. To anyone who didn't know, it was just a pretty key fob. It was, in the right hands, a weapon that could kill.

I took it from her, hefted it, nodded, and handed it back to her. She grinned at me.

"You hit him in the head with that?" I asked.

She nodded.

"It's a wonder you didn't kill him."

"Yes, I know, but he had me on my back. I managed to grab this from my pocket, and… I just swung it. I realized when he fell over backward that I might have hit him too hard but, as I was backing away, I saw him get up, so I turned and ran."

"Did you report him?" Kate asked.

"No. I was okay, and I didn't need the hassle I knew it would cause. He would have just denied it, and knowing him, it would have been me that attacked him, so I let it go. I haven't spoken to him since."

"He said he dated Maggie several times," I said. "Was that true?"

"If it was she never told me about it, but then she kept her sex life very much to herself."

"No girl talk?" Kate asked.

She shrugged. "What's girl talk? Some of the girls around here mate like rabbits. Then they brag about who, when, how, and how many times. You have no idea what goes on in the dorms. Some of us came here to study and others, well, you know. Maggie wasn't like that. Or if she was, I never saw it."

"But Joey," Kate said.

"I don't know. Like I said, if she did date him, she kept it to herself. Have you talked to Christie, her sister?"

"We have," I said. "What about Charles Elkins?"

"Charlie? Yeah right. I know he asked her out a few times because I heard him doing it. But again, if she ever said yes, I didn't know about it."

"And what about her ex, Bobby Haskins?" I asked.

She looked warily at me, then at Kate. "Yes," she said eventually. "He'd pick her up every now and then, take her for coffee, lunch, dinner once that I know of, you know."

"So they did date, then?" Kate asked.

She shook her head. "I told you, she kept all that to herself. I don't know. Maybe."

She was silent for a moment, obviously deep in thought, then said, "She *did* date. At least I think she did, because sometimes she came to class looking like hell, like she hadn't slept all night. If it was Bobby or not, I don't know. I didn't question her about it, other than asking her if she was okay. You couldn't. She was a closed book. I think something probably made her that way. What it was I don't know. We were friends almost before we could walk. Our moms were friends. She was an amazing kid. A great athlete. Man could she run. Then, one day—just after her sixteenth birthday—she changed. Not much. Not so much that anyone who didn't know her well would notice, but I did, and so did Christie. She became… secretive, I guess."

She was painting a picture of an enigma. *Just who the hell was Maggie Hart? Did she date or didn't she? Did something happen to her when she turned sixteen, I wonder? If so, what? We need to talk to Christie again.*

"You spent a lot of time with her, right?" I asked. "Was anything worrying her, do you think? Was she upset about anything? Had she had an argument with anyone?"

"Not that I know of. She seemed happy enough. Maybe she… I don't know. No, I'm trying to dig up stuff that isn't there. She was the way she always was. Studious, happy, my friend, and I loved her…." Her eyes began to water.

"Okay, Jessica," I said. "That'll do for now. You've been a great help. If we need to talk to you again, we'll call you. In the meantime, if you think of anything, anything at all, you can give me or Lieutenant Gazzara a call." I handed her my card, and Kate did the same, and then we left.

***

"What do you think?" I asked Kate when we got back to the car. I opened the driver's-side door for her. She rolled her eyes, but got in.

"I think we now have more questions than answers. Who the hell was she? From what we've heard, she had at least three different personas. I also got the feeling from what the guys said that she was more than a little loose with her affections, if not her body."

"True," I said, "But that's not the image you get from her female friends. We need to talk to the others, but… not today. I want to go back and dig into those files. See what we can learn from the other two victims. And I have to be home by five thirty; August and Rose are coming for dinner. It's now—" I looked at my watch "—just after three. That gives us a couple of hours. Let's go to your office. My car's there, so I can make a quick getaway." I grinned at her.

She nodded, hit the starter, put the car in drive, and eased away from the curb, out onto Vine and then right onto Douglas, and then we headed east.

Chapter 13

It was 3:15 when we walked into the incident room. I went to the whiteboard while Kate sent her photos to the printer. She joined me a few minutes later. She fixed the photos to the board in a column, one above the other—Elkins, Haskins, Lister, Christie Hart, Jessica Little. Then she stepped back, and we stood together and stared at the board. We were joined a minute or so later by Lonnie.

"How'd it go?" he asked.

Kate turned to look at him, shaking her head. "It's a riddle wrapped in a mystery inside an enigma."

"Winston Churchill, right?" I asked, without turning away from the board.

"Yeah, him, I guess. I dunno. Was it?"

"I think so. And you're right. That's exactly what this is." I grabbed a dry-erase marker and stepped toward the board. "Bobby Haskins has a blue and white, 1974 Ford F100 pickup…." I said, writing the word *truck* beside his photo.

"No way," Lonnie said incredulously.

"Yeah, way," I said. "Better yet, it has tinted windows, *and* he admits to her having been in the truck on numerous occasions, so any prints, trace, or DNA we find, unless we find her blood, is useless. He also denies seeing her that evening, but unless someone saw him at Zazby's, he has no alibi for the time Maggie went missing. So he has a truck of the right year and model, with tinted windows, and we can place the victim in the truck. Coincidence? Could be, but I don't like it."

"Me neither," Lonnie said. "It's gotta be him. Let's haul his ass in here and go for a confession."

"Let's not," I said. "First, no, it doesn't *have* to be him. It's all circumstantial. It could be just as he explained. Her sister told us that they'd had a nasty breakup, but Bobby told us he was still seeing her. We know from what her best friend Jessica Little told us that that was at least partially true, that Bobby and Maggie remained friends and often spent time together. Whether or not they dated… we don't know."

I stared up at Bobby's photo. He looked devastated. "Kate," I said, "we need to hear from Foote and Holtz."

She nodded, took out her phone, and tapped in a text message. "So," she said, tucking the phone away again, "Haskins is our best bet, but Harry, I don't know. It's too easy. And I don't think he has it in him."

"Ah, maybe you're right. But I think we're all pretty much in agreement that the three killings are connected, but as to how and why…. We need to figure out the motive, and that's not going to be easy. Serial killers operate on a totally different wavelength than normal killers. And we need to find the actual crime scene. We know he keeps them alive, right?" I looked at her.

She nodded. So did Lonnie.

"So where the hell is he keeping them? It has to be secluded. You can't just drag someone out of a vehicle in the center of town. It would too risky. Someone would be sure to see him."

Kate looked doubtful. "If it was dark…."

"I don't think so. Even a nut job would think twice about it. It has to be a house… with a basement, a garage even, or somewhere with a driveway, so he could get off the street. Elkins is a registered sex offender and has no alibi, but he doesn't have the juice, I can tell. Haskins also has no alibi, other than Zaxby's, but he lives with his mother. That by itself would tend to rule him out, but more than that, that house doesn't have a garage or even a large shed. Joey Lister, according to Jessica Little, is potentially a rapist, but he does have an alibi for the afternoon Maggie was abducted and he doesn't own a pickup that we know of. We need to check that alibi, though."

"Elkins's place does have a driveway up the side of the house," Kate said, "and a back entrance. But you're right that his mother's the problem." She was silent for a moment. "Maybe he has a storage unit somewhere?"

"Are you serious?" Lonnie asked. "Those things are made of sheet metal. The slightest sound would attract attention. We can find out if he has one, but I don't see it. Not a storage unit."

She shrugged. "Maybe you're right, but there are plenty of abandoned plants scattered around the city. As you know only too well, Harry."

She was right, I did, and much to my regret.

"There are some off Amnicola that are almost within walking distance of the Riverwalk. He could have found himself a hidey-hole somewhere.

I nodded. "It's worth looking into. Why don't you have one of the clerks do a search of the storage companies, see if they can come up with anything."

"I suggest we put a tail on that Haskins son of a bitch, too," Lonnie said.

"That too," I agreed. "Do you have the manpower, Kate?"

"I think I can persuade the chief to turn loose some uniforms for a couple of days. Any more than that and we'd better be able to justify it. Gimme a sec."

The call didn't last long, and when she hung up she was smiling grimly.

"He says we can have six officers; three shifts of two. No overtime. Lonnie," she said, "go meet them and tell them what we need: twenty-four-hour surveillance of Haskins. I want to know his every move."

He nodded. "Will do."

"So, what about this character?" I tapped the tip of the dry-erase marker on Joey Lister's photo. "He's a nasty piece of work, has his brains in his crotch. Thinks he's God's gift to women, or at least that's how Jessica described him. She also said he tried to rape her. If that's true, and I have no reason to doubt it, he's psychopathic at best, and maybe a whole lot worse. He's a frat boy: wealthy family, entitled, violent. He says he dated the vic a few times. No one seems to know if that's actually true or just braggadocio. If it was true, Maggie didn't tell anyone. His alibi, if it holds up, would eliminate him though, so it needs checking out.

"Lonnie, when you're done with the uniforms, that's what you'll do. He said he was with a… Jennifer Lockerby from six until seven thirty at the Bonefish Grill. She lives on campus, so she'll be easy enough to run down. The Bonefish, if he paid with a credit card, should have a time-stamped receipts. Shouldn't take more than a couple of hours, right?"

He nodded. "I'll get on it." He started to get to his feet, but I waved him back down.

"No, not right now. Stay until we're done with this, at least. You might get some ideas. Then you can go. So, moving on to Charlie Elkins." I scribbled a big question mark against his photo. "I don't know about this guy. He has no alibi. Says he beat the shit out of Bobby; Bobby says it was the other way around. Christie, the sister, claims that he was the vic's guardian angel, but everyone else seems to think that all he wanted was to get into her pants. When asked if he'd ever dated Maggie, he answered no—a little too quickly, I thought. He said that she wasn't his type. And, like I said, he's got no alibi, so I have to wonder. Kate?"

She was seated on the edge of the table, her arms folded and her legs crossed at the ankles. She was staring up at the photo of Maggie Hart.

"I keep coming back to that blue and white truck," she said. "There aren't that many of them around these days, and the tinted windows.... You rarely ever see an old-model truck with those. Yeah, I know it's a ten-minute job to have it done, but why would you, unless you had something to hide?"

She had a point.

"I'm thinking Lonnie may be right," she continued. "Maybe we should bring Haskins in, talk to him."

"Yeah," Lonnie said. "We should."

I nodded slowly, thinking. "Maybe, but let's not act too quickly; let's wait a little. I'd like to go through the files on the other two women first. Maybe there's something in them that we're not seeing."

I stared up at Maggie Hart's photo, then Jasmine Payne's, and finally Dana Walters's. I was trying find some physical attribute that might link them together. They were all lovely, but different: Maggie Hart was five foot nine, blonde, and wore her hair short. Jasmine Payne was five foot three and a redhead. Dana Walters was five foot six and brunette. Maggie was slim, athletic. The other two were of medium build. I shook my head. I had a feeling I was in for another rough night.

"I know I said we agreed, but I'm still not entirely sure," I said. "I'm not seeing a connection. I know what you think, Kate, and the causes of death would tend to support the theory, and I'm leaning that way myself, but *these* three?" I shook my head, then turned and looked at her.

She just shrugged.

"Okay Lonnie." I turned back to the board. "Have at it. Go organize the surveillance, and then check out Lister's alibi. Let us know what you find."

He made some notes and headed out the door.

"Kate, let's go to your office and talk about the other two victims."

We sat opposite each other, Kate behind her desk, me in front of it. I had Jasmine Payne's case file open across my knees.

"We need to dig into these other two victims," I said. "There has to be something that connects them. I have a feeling that maybe Joey Lister knew at least one of them, and I'm not sure but I think Elkins might have too; maybe even both of them. And Bobby, he would have been around when they were killed. In fact, all three of them would have been, but let me ask you this: Why would they do it? What possible motive could any one of these three have to kill all three girls? Maggie, yeah, I can see that. But the others? I don't know, and that's what's bothering me. I'm thinking we should concentrate on Maggie Hart. The others have gone cold. I'm thinking that if we can solve Maggie's murder, we might solve the others too."

She stared at me across the desk, her eyes narrowed. "That sounds reasonable, but my gut is telling me it's the ex-boyfriend, Bobby Haskins. Like you, I don't believe in coincidences, and there are just too many. I want to bring him in."

I nodded. "I know you do, but like I said, let's wait for Mike Willis, okay?"

She nodded, but I could see she wasn't convinced.

"Look," I said, "We know all three were killed somewhere else and then moved. We know Bobby had the means to do that, and he could have done it. Right now he's our prime suspect. Maybe he has a motive—jealousy perhaps, or the 'If I can't have her, nobody can' thing.

"Lister's a creepy bastard. I could see him killing Maggie and, if he's a rapist, maybe even the others. He has a Nissan Rogue: hardly enough room for a body, but it could be done, except the Rogue doesn't fit the scene on the night Maggie was abducted.

"Elkins is an enigma. He has a Bronco, one of the big, full-size models. That would be big enough.... a 1985... model. Hey Kate, that model-year Bronco looks a lot like a pickup with a camper on the back, and his is blue and white.... You don't think the witness could have been mistaken... could she?"

"Hm. Maybe. I'll have Foote pull up some pics and go have her take another look.... Harry, I've just sat here for the last ten minutes listening to you make the case that the killings might or might not be connected, and also that any one of the three could have killed Maggie, and that one of them might well have killed all three. I'm worse off than I was before you arrived."

I grinned at her. "Yeah. Sorry about that, but don't worry. We'll get there."

The look she gave me was one of... total frustration.

"So," I said, "let's say they're connected. Let's talk about that, about them. Jasmine Payne was twenty-two years old and, like Maggie Hart, lived in one of the dorms on campus. She was a psychology major, disappeared on July tenth and was found dead on July fifteenth. She'd been dead for three days and strangled multiple times, just like Maggie Hart. Also like Maggie, she was found on the Riverwalk. The cause of death and the location would seem to indicate that two deaths are connected."

I looked up at Kate. Her lips were tight, her eyes half closed; she was listening intently.

I continued. "Payne was last seen leaving her apartment—by her roommate—to go to the library to study. When she hadn't returned by the following morning, the roommate reported her missing." I looked up again and said, "No boyfriends, didn't date, spent all her time studying. In fact, it says here that she was taking some private, summer tutoring, hoping to graduate early. There's not a whole lot more we know about her, Kate."

"You're right. There isn't anything more to tell. She only had a few friends and no one saw her after she left her dorm. If she arrived at the library, no one saw her, but that's not unusual. The library is huge, with plenty of places to hide away and enjoy a quiet hour or two with the books."

"What about her tutor, this professor, Dr. David Greenwood?" I asked. "I don't see a record of an interview."

"Well, he's an older guy, English. I spoke to him briefly; he seemed very nice, a bit… scatterbrained? His mind was completely on other things. He did say that she'd missed her first two scheduled appointments and that he hadn't seen her since the last day of class, which I think was June seventeenth."

"How about Dana Walters?" I asked.

"She was barely nineteen. She was strangled only once, that we know of, but she wasn't found on the Riverwalk. It looked like a random sex crime…. Look, I told you I didn't get that case until Lonnie found it among the missing persons files. It's been designated a cold case. There's nothing there really, except that she was also a student at UTC, a year ahead of the other two girls."

I nodded. "What was her major?"

"Psychology, with a minor in American history."

I raised my eyebrows.

She nodded. "Yes, she had Dr. Greenwood too."

"Did you talk to Maggie's professors?"

She nodded. "Yes, a Mr. Douglas Wiggins had her for both art and art history. He had nothing to add."

"Hmmm. So we have two psychology majors—same professor—and an art major. That doesn't help much."

I sighed, closed the files, and looked at my watch. It was just after four thirty. Time for me to go.

"How about I take this stuff home with me again tonight," I said. "We can take up where we left off in the morning. That good for you?"

"Sure. I'll wait to hear from Lonnie and from Stop and Go. If there's anything you need to know, I'll call you, but if not, I see you here at… eight thirty tomorrow morning?"

"Yeah, eight thirty…. Stop and Go? Ohhhh, I get it. Holtz and Foote. I like that. Good one, Kate."

I smiled and shook my head as I got up out of my seat. I looked at her across her desk. She cocked her head, smiled at me, and winked. It was a look I remembered well, from the days when… ah, but that's a whole 'nother story.

The Beast—my Camaro ZL1—was parked at the rear of the PD building, and when I saw it I had the distinct feeling it was waiting for me, crouched low on the pavement like a great gray cat. When I bought it I hadn't been sure it was the right thing to do, but over the past couple of months it had kinda grown on me. There were now a few more of them on the streets, less expensive models, but still not more than a half dozen like mine, and none the same color, Nighthawk Gray.

I sank into the leather seat and leaned against the backrest and let it enfold me and, for the first time that day, I actually relaxed. I hit the starter and the great engine burst into life, then the growl subsided, and the car grumbled softly. I sat quietly for a minute, enjoying Beethoven's *Für Elise* on satellite radio and thinking.

Are they connected? Seems likely... but I don't see it. Those three kids? Nah.... Through Lister, though? Maybe. If he's a rapist. Except he doesn't have a truck. Seemed anxious to let me know he wouldn't be seen dead in one... so he could actually have one. And he knew Jasmine, that I'm certain of.

But what about Bobby? Boy does he have problems. Elkins? Bronco? Right color. No alibi. Liar. They all *could have killed Maggie, but I don't see Bobby or Elkins doing all three.... That little shit Lister, though. In fact, the more I think about it.... Yeah.... Yeah!*

I slipped the Beast into reverse and then into drive and slowly eased out onto Amnicola. I headed downtown, onto Broad Street and then up Lookout Mountain, my mind on other things. It wasn't until I turned onto Scenic Parkway halfway up the mountain that I realized I had no idea of how I'd gotten there. I remembered absolutely nothing of the drive to that point, and that shook me. Yes, I know, we all have moments like that. But at the wheel of a 620-horsepower animal that would be more at home at Daytona than on the streets of Chattanooga… it wasn't good.

By the time I made it into the garage, I'd come to the conclusion that the Beast had to go. It was just too much car for me.

I found Amanda in the kitchen with my father, August, and my stepmother, Rose, waiting for me. I hate the term "stepmother," and wouldn't use it except that Rose is twenty years younger than my dad, and just three years older than me. She's a beautiful woman: tall, blonde, perfect skin, perfect figure. The talk around the club is that she married my father for his money. If she did, I haven't seen any evidence of it. She's been called, more than once, the "quintessential trophy wife," but she's not. She's actually very kind, and I *know* she loves my old man dearly. I love her for that, and would defend her to the death.

Anyway, that being said, my little family was now all in one place, my younger half brother, Henry, having passed almost two years before. That's another story too.

Amanda gave me a quick kiss, then I hugged my dad and kissed Rose on the cheek.

"So why are we here, Harry?" August asked.

August Starke, my father, is an attorney, sixty-seven years old with a head of thick, silver hair and an attitude that screams, "Don't screw around with me." He's one of those larger than life figures with a voice that dominates any room he walks into, lounge bar or courtroom. He's the most competitive man I've ever met, and one of the country's top lawyers. He also has more money than Croesus.

"Does there have to be a reason?" I asked. "Maybe we just thought it would be nice to see you and Rose outside the confines of the club."

He snorted. "Son, I know you better than that. What's going on?"

"Later," I replied. "Right now I need a shower and drink, in reverse order."

Amanda handed me the drink, a triple shot of Laphroaig with a single lump of ice, and I headed for the bedroom and the shower.

I rejoined them some thirty minutes later. I poured myself another drink, then sat down on the sofa next to Amanda and took her hand in mine. The furniture in my living room had been arranged to take full advantage of one of the most beautiful views in Tennessee, if not the country. August was seated in an easy chair to my right, Rose in another to my left.

I sipped on my drink, squeezed Amanda's hand, and gazed out over the city and the great river, enjoying the moment. August, however, had had enough.

"Oh come *on,* boy. Why the hell have you dragged us up this damn mountain? We could be eating dinner at the club, for Christ's sake."

I looked at Amanda.

"We're going to have a baby," she said.

Rose gasped. From my old man, nothing but stunned silence, and then: "About damned time. Is that it? Can we go to dinner now?"

I thought Amanda would be wounded, but instead she burst out laughing, jumped up, ran to him, wrapped her arms around his neck, and squeezed until his face turned red.

"You wicked old man," she said affectionately.

"Oh get the hell off me, woman…." And then he did something I'd never seen him do before. Slowly he wrapped his arms around her and said, barely loud enough for me to hear, "I love you too, Amanda, and I'm so happy for you both." Then he pushed her away, "*Now* can we go to dinner?" And we did.

We went to the club, and August insisted on buying, not just the meal, but drinks for any and all who ventured into the lounge or dining room. I dread to think what his bar bill must have been that night, but he seemed not to care. I know I sure didn't, and I don't think I'd seen him so happy in a very long time. He'd been… very quiet since Henry passed.

Amanda and I arrived home right around eleven o'clock, and I'm ashamed to have to tell you that, for the second night in a row, I was unable to get to the files. I felt bad about it, but what the hell. For the first time in my life I dared to believe that, at the great age of forty-seven, I was going to become a father. And it felt good.

The night ended for Amanda and me with a midnight swim and then…. Well, use your imagination.

***

I woke, sweating like a pig, at exactly three o'clock in the morning. Panicked, I looked to my left. Amanda was gone, but I wasn't alone. They were there, all three of them, standing beside the bed dressed in white shifts, their faces as pale as alabaster, staring down at me. I tried to speak. I could form the words, but my mouth moved silently.

Maggie shook her head. She looked disappointed. Then, she leaned forward and placed her hand on my shoulder. I flinched at her touch. Her hand was cold. I shuddered, closed my eyes, opened them again. The girls were gone. I looked to my left. Amanda was curled up beside me, snoring softly. I'd been dreaming… right? The cold sensation in my right shoulder… it still lingered. I looked up into the dark corner of the cathedral ceiling, but there was nothing, just the dim outline of the wooden beams.

Amanda stirred, stretched, rolled over onto her back, her eyes half open.

"What time is it?" she whispered sleepily.

"Early. Go back to sleep. Everything's fine."

And I lay back, and stared up into the shadows.

The next thing I knew, my alarm was chirping. It was six o'clock. Tomorrow had become today.

Chapter 14

That morning I decided to forego my run in favor of laps in the pool. Fifty fast laps later I was back in the house, showered and ready to face the day.

I took my coffee to the breakfast bar, turned on the TV, and flipped to Channel 7, just in time to hear the anchor say, "Sources close to the investigation told our reporter that the police are convinced that the two murders, and possibly a third, are linked.... Both victims were apparently strangled multiple times." I listened to the rest of the report. It was all speculation and spin, but damaging just the same.

Damn it! Who the hell...?

I called Kate.

"You're watching the news, right?" she asked before I could get a word out.

"Yeah. It would seem that we—make that you—have a leak in the department. That's not good. Kate. We need to keep it out of the media, especially my role in the investigation."

"Ehhh, it's a bit late for that, I think. It was on the late news last night too. I saw it myself on Channel 6. Your name came up a few times."

"Ah hell," I interrupted her. "That's bad, Kate. I wanted to keep a low profile."

"Yeah, well. Good luck with that. I'll see you at eight thirty?"

“Yep. Eight thirty.” I disconnected, picked up my cup, and stared out of the widow. The sky was an unbroken field of blue, the sun a great golden ball just above the horizon. A light mist from the river shrouded the city below. I sighed.

“Hey,” Amanda said.

I turned and looked her. She was wearing one of my T-shirts and had obviously just crawled out of bed. She put both hands on my left shoulder and laid her head on top of them. “You didn’t bring me coffee,” she mumbled.

“No, I didn’t; sorry. Go sit down. I’ll get you some.” She did.

I handed her the cup, sat down beside her, and waited for her to shake off the fugue. “Someone leaked details about the case to the media,” I said eventually. “It’s on your station this morning. Did you know?”

She looked at me and nodded. “I recused myself and asked them to keep your name out of it. I was promised they would.”

“You didn’t tell me?”

“No.”

“Why not?”

She shrugged. “Telling you wouldn’t change anything, and I didn’t want to spoil the evening.”

“You didn’t think I needed to know?”

"Harry. I learned a long time ago not to worry about the things I couldn't change." Again the shrug.

"So where did it come from, the information?"

She looked sideways at me. "I don't know… and you know I wouldn't tell you if I did. Sources are confidential—always."

"I need to know, Amanda. It's important we stop the leak."

"I told you, I couldn't tell you even if I knew." She paused, looked at me over the rim of her cup, then asked, "So you think there's a serial killer?"

I looked at her. She raised her eyebrows.

I hesitated, then said, "I don't know, maybe…. Look, Amanda, you can't use *anything* I tell you."

She nodded. "Do you have a suspect?"

I stared out across the city, then, reluctantly, "Yeah. We do."

"And?"

"And nothing. You know better than to ask."

She nodded, thought for a minute, then said, "You woke me up last night. What was that about?"

"A bad dream. I've had it three nights in a row. It seemed so real."

"You want to tell me about it?"

I didn't, but I told her anyway. When I'd finished, she just stared at me. I knew just what she was thinking. I have this… not clairvoyance exactly, but sometimes a scary sort of sixth sense. It's dogged me all my adult life, and it's not always helpful.

"What does it mean, d'you think?" she asked finally.

"I don't know. Probably nothing."

"You don't think they're trying to tell you something?"

"Oh come on, Amanda. It was a *dream*, for God's sake."

"Yes, well. You would know."

She was right. I would. And I did. And I didn't like it.

I stood up. "I have to go. I'll be late."

She put her cup down, wrapped her arms around my neck, kissed me gently, then looked at me and said, "They're good people, Harry. You should listen to them."

"Who?"

"The people in the dream."

***

I'm usually a stickler for punctuality. My father brought me up with the idea that to keep someone waiting was to show a lack of respect for that person and their time. I know I sure as hell hate being kept waiting. So I was kind of mad at myself for being late that morning.

When I finally made it into the situation room at the police department, it was almost nine o'clock, and Kate wasn't happy. I made my apologies, grabbed a cup of coffee, and joined her and Lonnie in her office.

"Nice of you to join us," she said dryly, as I took the vacant seat in front of her desk.

"Hey, it couldn't be helped and I've apologized, so let's get on with it, shall we? And how about we begin with the damned leak in your department? My name is out there *again.* That's not what I signed on for."

She glared at me across the desk. "You don't know it came from here. It could have been that clown Lister, and you let that cat out."

I glared back at her. Oh I was pissed, and even more so when she reminded me that I had indeed presented Joey with Jasmine Payne's name.

"Well," I said. "It's done. Now we have to live with it and I suggest we take control and do our own leaking from now on. Other than Amanda and—" I sighed and shook my head "—and Charlie Grove, I don't trust any of them."

She nodded thoughtfully. "We can keep just the two of them updated. Or give it a try, anyway. Why don't you set up a meeting… actually no, not yet. Let's wait till we know a little more."

I nodded. "So," I said to Lonnie, "what about Lister's alibi? Does it hold up?"

He grinned. “Not hardly. Yeah, Lister was there at the Bonefish all right—”

Damn!

“—but on that Tuesday, not Wednesday.”

I gaped at him, hardly able to believe it. “Are you sure?”

“Oh yeah. I have the original receipt with his signature on it Tuesday, August twenty-ninth.” He handed it over. “Check out the date and time stamp. He paid with a Visa at 7:12. Unless he has an alibi for the next day, he’s swingin’ in the wind.”

I looked at Kate. “One down, two to go. How about Haskins? Have you heard from Foote and Holtz?”

“Yep. If Haskins was at Zaxby’s that day, no one remembers seeing him. We just have his word for it.”

“Two down, then,” I said. “Why don’t you see how Mike Willis is doing with Bobby Haskins’s truck? He should be done with it soon.”

She called him. “He’s done. He’s on his way up, shouldn’t be—” she glanced out the office window “—oh, and there he is.” She stood, opened the door, and waited.

“Hey Mike,” she said as he walked towards her. “We need another chair. Grab one and bring it with you.”

When he came into the room he was carrying a thin file under one arm and a chair under the other. He dropped the chair between Lonnie and me, sat down heavily, and tossed the file on Kate's desk.

"That copy is for you. You probably should send someone to go get him. There'd been zero attempt to clean the truck, which gives me some doubts—if he did this thing, you'd think he would have made some attempt to clean the vehicle, but he didn't, and the girl's prints, along with a variety of others, are plastered all over the inside of the truck and on the outside of the passenger side door; there are even some on the passenger side box sides. I found eleven blonde hairs that look like a match—won't know until we get DNA results back, which could take a month. I also found three dark brown hairs.

"Folks." He paused for effect, looked around at each of us in turn, then said, "I also found a tiny smear of blood on the inside of the passenger side door. Again, we'll have to wait for the DNA results, but it's the same blood group as the victim's, O-negative. It's not the rarest group, but it is scarce; only one in ten people have it, so...." He paused, flipped the page, and went on.

"We don't have a match on any of the prints except Margaret Hart's, but I sent the hairs to the DNA lab. It's another long shot, but you never know."

I leaned back in my chair and laced my fingers together behind my neck. Mike's report was everything I'd expected it would be, except for the blood.

I looked at Kate. She stared back at me, lips tight, eyes narrowed.

"It's time to bring him in," she said quietly.

I thought about it, then nodded reluctantly.

"Yep," I said. "You're right, but don't get your hopes up. We knew what we were going to find. Haskins told us. The only game changer is the blood, and right now that means nothing."

"True, but I'll feel a whole lot better when he's here, where he can do no harm."

"You're going to *charge* him?"

She shrugged. "We'll see."

She picked her iPhone up and tapped in a number, then put the phone to her ear. "Tommy? Good. Take Sarah with you and go pick up Robert Haskins and bring him in. Ask him to come in voluntarily. Just tell him we just need to get answers to a few questions, nothing else. If he argues, tell him you'll arrest him. That's right. Uh-huh. Yeah. As soon as you can. Let me know when you get here."

"Well," Mike said, rising to his feet. "You know where you can find me."

Before he could leave though, there was a knock at the door. It opened, and one of clerks leaned in, her hand extended toward me.

"Sorry to interrupt, Lieutenant, but this was hand-delivered to the front desk. It's for Mr. Starke. It's marked as urgent."

She handed the large brown envelope to me and left. I turned it over and looked at the back. Other than my name printed in black, and the word *Urgent*, it was unmarked: no return address, nothing.

I held it up to the light. Nothing. By now, all three of them were watching me.

"Lonnie," I said. "Go grab her and find out exactly where this came from."

He got up and left.

"Do you have gloves in your desk, Kate?" I asked.

She looked puzzled, but she slid open a drawer and took out a small box of latex gloves.

I grabbed a pair and put them on. "Knife?"

She took a small pocketknife from her desk organizer, opened it, and handed it to me. Carefully, I slit the seal and opened the envelope, looked inside, and then extracted a single sheet of white printer paper. I set the empty envelope down on the desk and stared at the piece of paper. It was blank, on both sides… except for a large yellow emoji outlined in black. It was maybe three by four inches. The face bore a mocking smile, but that wasn't all. It also had hands. They were palms up with the fingers curled, beckoning, as if to say, *Bring it on.*

I looked up at Kate. "Well. Obviously this is from the killer. He must have been watching the local news last night or this morning and knows I'm involved. This is a friggin' challenge."

I handed her the piece of paper. She put on a glove and took it by the corner, between the tips of two fingers, stared at it, turned it over, stared some more, looked at me, then at Mike, and finally she shook her head.

"Christ," she said. "Is this for real?"

"Oh it's real," I said.

It was at that moment that Lonnie returned.

"It was left at the front desk," he said, "by a guy. She didn't see him, but the receptionist did. She didn't take a whole lot of notice of him, but figured him to be between twenty-five and thirty-five, maybe a little older, wearing a cowboy hat. The cameras in the lobby have him, but just for a couple of seconds, and the hat hid his face. He was driving a pickup truck. He parked outside the front door and ran in. Handed it to her, told her it was for you, then dashed out. She could see the truck outside the front door; said it was a light green color, teal." He grinned as he sat down, then nodded at the piece of paper. "Is that it?"

She nodded.

"What is it?"

"We don't know."

"Do we know who sent it?"

"Nope."

"A light green pickup?" I asked. "Did she get the make and model?"

"Nah, but she did say it was pretty old, and that it needed a paint job."

I shook my head. "This is not happening." I looked at Lonnie. "Teal? She was sure?"

He nodded.

"Jeez!" I said. "Friggin' *teal?* Are you kidding me? That's only one or two shades removed from light blue, for Christ's sake. What the hell is going on? And what the hell is that all about?" I waved my hand at the emoji paper still in Kate's hand.

"Mike," I said, turning to Willis. "I know it's going to be a total waste of time, because you're not going to find a damned thing, but you need to process that—" I nodded at the piece of paper "—and the envelope, ASAP. Like right now, please. And Mike. I hope it goes without saying that you keep this thing to yourself."

He grabbed a pair of latex gloves from Kate's box, slipped them on, took the piece of paper and the envelope from her, and said, "I'll get right on it. You never know, some smartasses aren't quite as smart as they think they are…. Damn. It's a self-sealer, so no saliva. Bummer."

He closed the door behind him when he left. The room was quiet. None of us quite knew where to begin.

"Kate," I said finally. "We can't let this happen. If that emoji came from the killer, he's already escalating; now he's looking for immortality, for notoriety. If he hasn't already, he's going to kill again. We have to find him. If it's just some clown playing games, which I hope to God it is, I can live with that, but we still need to put a stop to it."

"But the pickup, Harry," she said quietly. That rules Haskins out. Mike still has his."

"No, it doesn't. Not yet. Right now, we have to assume the emoji is the result of last night's newscast. That someone's screwing with us, having fun at our—my—expense."

"So you don't think it was our killer, then?"

"I don't know. But we have to keep this emoji thing from the media. If they get hold of it, they'll have a field day."

"Mm. So what now?"

"We wait for them to bring Haskins in. Then we rip him a new one. We either find a reason to charge him or we eliminate him. Right now, though, I don't see how the hell we can charge him."

"Okay," Lonnie said suddenly, "I've been thinking. Let's say it was him, Bobby Haskins, who picked her up that evening. It doesn't necessarily mean he was the last person to see her alive. He could have dropped her off at the parking lot on the greenway and left her there… but… why would she have him do that?"

Kate and I smiled grimly at him.

"Go on," Kate said.

"She wouldn't, would she?" he asked. "She'd need to know she had a ride home. Whoever picked her up had to be her killer."

"That's the way I see it," I said.

"So she must have known him," Lonnie said, thoughtfully. "Had to have. It's Bobby Haskins. Has to be. Did he know any of the other vics, I wonder?"

"Me too," I said. "Me too."

Chapter 15

It was just after eleven thirty when they brought Robert Haskins in. He had come voluntarily, so they settled him into an interview room and gave him a Coke.

We watched him through the one-way glass for several minutes before entering the room. He was noticeably nervous, though not excessively so.

We decided that Kate would do the interview and that I would observe, jumping in with questions if I needed to; Lonnie would watch through the one-way glass.

"Hey Bobby," Kate said, sitting down on one of the two chairs opposite him—I took the other. "Thank you for agreeing to come in and talk to us."

"I didn't think I had a choice," he said.

"Yes, of course you did. In fact, you can leave right now if you want. However, if you do…."

"It's okay," he said. "I don't mind, but I need to get back to work. I can't afford to lose—"

"Good," Kate interrupted. "We'll get you out of here as quick as we can. Now, just to keep things straight, I'm informing you that this interview is being recorded. Is that okay with you?"

He nodded.

"Speak up, Bobby. For the record, please."

He looked her in the eye and said, "Yes. That's okay. Are you going to tell me my rights?"

"I hadn't planned on it," she said. "You're not under arrest; this is just an informal chat."

"If it's informal, why are you recording it?"

"Like I told you, Bobby, it's for the record. To protect you and us."

"Okay," he said slowly, obviously not quite buying it, but not sure enough to make a fuss. "How can I help?"

"Let's talk about your truck," Kate said casually.

His eyes flickered from her to me and then back again. He didn't answer.

"Bobby?" she asked.

"Yeah, okay, what about it?"

She looked down at her iPad. "Well, we have the report back from forensics and it was pretty much the way you said it would be. We found Maggie's fingerprints all over it, inside and out, and we found some hairs which we think are probably hers, but…." She paused, looked again at her tablet. I watched his face. He waited. He had this tick thing going at the corners of his mouth.

Stress? Maybe.

Finally, she looked up at him and said, "Bobby, we found blood in the cab, her blood, on the passenger side door."

Whoa, Kate. That's a bit of a stretch. We don't know that for sure yet.

He was nodding. "Yeah, under the door handle, right? She'd tripped coming down the steps and skinned her knuckle on the brick wall."

"When was that, Bobby?" Kate asked.

"I dunno, last week? A few days before she…. It was lunchtime. I took her to Panera's. Monday. It was Monday last week."

"And which hand?" Kate asked.

"Her right. It was the knuckle of her middle finger. I know 'cause she couldn't get the Band-Aid I gave her on right and I had to do it for her."

I took my phone from my pocket and texted Doc Sheddon,

Hey Doc. Is there any sign of a scrape on Maggie Hart's right hand?

The answer came back almost immediately. *Yes, knuckle, middle finger.*

I held the phone for Kate to see. She nodded.

"Bobby," she said, "I don't want you to get upset, but I have to ask you, do you know either of these two girls?"

She laid two 8x10 prints down side-by-side in front of him. He leaned forward, gripped the edge of the table with both hands, and stared down at them.

"No…. No, I don't think so. She looks familiar." He pointed to the photo of Jasmine Payne. "But I don't know her. I don't know either of them. Why? Are they…?"

"Are they what?" Kate asked.

He didn't get a chance to answer. I was in the process of stuffing my phone back into my pocket when it buzzed. I had another text. It was from Amanda.

Call me ASAP. Urgent.

I nudged Kate and showed her the text. She nodded, pushed her seat back, and stood.

"Bobby," she said. "We need to take a short break. If you need the restroom, now would be a good time. The officer will take you."

He said he didn't need it.

"I wouldn't have bothered you," I said to Kate when we got outside, "but Amanda's at the station and she wouldn't do this if something wasn't up."

I made the call.

Amanda answered on the second ring. "Whew," she said. "What I have to tell you is going to upset you a *lot*."

"Wait," I said. "Kate's here. Does she need to hear this?"

"Yes, I think maybe she does."

"Okay, hold on while I put you on speaker…. Okay, go."

"Fifteen minutes ago," she began. "Jamie at the news desk took a call. The caller wouldn't give his name. Said he was with the police department. I don't know if he was or not.... Harry, did you receive a package this morning?"

Oh shit. Here we go!

I hesitated, looked at Kate. She shrugged, then nodded.

"Ye-es," I said.

"What was in it?"

"I can't tell you that, Amanda. It's part of the investigation."

"Well, let me tell you then. It was an envelope addressed to you. Inside was a single piece of paper with an emoji on it."

I didn't answer. I looked at Kate. Her face was pale with anger.

"I take it from your silence that I'm right," Amanda said. "The caller went on to say that you, Harry, are investigating three cases, murders, all of them connected, and that you were convinced they are serial killings and that you'd named the killer… *Emoji."*

"Oh for Christ's sake, Amanda," I exploded. None of that's true… well, some, maybe, but Emoji? No, damnit, *no.*"

"Harry, he texted a copy of the emoji to the news desk. The team's going to run with this on the midday newscast. Jamie said he demanded that I do it, but I told them I couldn't. That it would be a conflict of interest."

"Wait," I said. "Stop."

"What?"

"You said the guy demanded that you run it," I said. "That doesn't sound like something a cop would do. It must have been him, the killer. Amanda," I said, "you have to stop them. This can't get out. It's exactly what he wants. He's playing you, playing me. For Christ's sake don't let them run it."

"I can't, Harry. He said if we didn't run it as the lead story, he would call the other three networks and give it to them in time for them to run it before the midday newscast will end."

"Oh jeez.... Damn, damn, *damn!* This is not happening. Hold on for a minute, will you? I need to talk to Kate." I took her off speaker.

"What the hell do we do now?" I asked Kate. She was smiling. "*What*?"

"Boy, do you looked pissed. Get over it, Harry. It's done. There's nothing we can do about it. And we can't deny it. If we do.... Well, you know the media; they'll hang us for it. He, whoever he is, has tossed us a hornet's nest. We have to run with it, and it would be best if Amanda handles it rather than the others. We can trust her to play it down."

I thought for a minute, nodded, and turned the speaker back on.

"Okay," I said. "But with two conditions. One, you do the story. Two, you run it by me and Kate before you go on the air."

"Harry!"

"I know, I know. We just want a heads up, that's all, and to make sure nothing's been added that shouldn't be."

She was silent for a minute, then said, "You can look at it, fact check it, but you're not going to rewrite the news. I won't let you."

"And I wouldn't have it any other way. Send it to me, please?"

"Five minutes, okay? It's not quite ready yet."

A few minutes later the fax spat out a single sheet of paper. I read what was written on it, shook my head, and handed it to Kate.

She read it, looked at me, rolled her eyes, and said, "This is going to cause a shit storm, but it is what it is. Tell her to go with it. I'll call the chief and tell him to watch the news. Better he gets it from me than an 'anonymous source,' right?"

I nodded and made the call. Kate called the chief. I found Lonnie coming out of the john and had him join us.

There was a small TV on top of a filing cabinet in Kate's office, so I grabbed the remote and turned it on, and we waited through an interminable number of commercials.

Finally, there she was. Amanda was wearing her signature outfit, a red blazer over a white dress. She looked stunning and… serious.

"Good afternoon. Please stand by." She waited for her co-anchor to hand her a piece of paper. Hah! Oh the drama.

"We have breaking news," she continued, setting the piece of paper down. It was, after all, just a prop. The story was rolling on the teleprompter. "A source close to the investigation into the death of UTC student, Margaret Hart, has just told us that the police are investigating the suspicious deaths of not just one, but three young women, all of them students at UTC. The source also stated that police are convinced that they are dealing with a serial killer whom they're calling Emoji. Why Emoji? Apparently a somewhat provocative graphic—you can see it at the lower right of your screen—was delivered earlier today to Private Investigator Harry Starke, who has been called in as a consultant on the investigation. This is not the first time that Starke has been involved in police business. A former police officer himself with more than seventeen years of experience, Starke is well known to the local community. He was, as you will recall, instrumental in bringing down Congressman Gordon Harper, among others.

"We reached out to Mr. Starke, and to Lieutenant Catherine Gazzara who is leading the investigation.

Neither would comment as the investigation is ongoing, but neither did they deny that the information provided by the anonymous source is true. That's all the information we have at this moment, but we'll be sure to update you as we learn more." She paused, and then continued, "In the early hours this morning, police were called to the scene of a drive-by shooting in—"

I flipped the TV off and sat back in my chair and looked at Kate. "Well. That's friggin' done it. Stand by for the hurricane… and here he is."

The door slammed open and Chief Johnston entered, much like that proverbial blast of wind.

"What the hell was that?" Boy was he angry. "Couldn't you friggin' stop it, Starke? She's your damned wife, for Christ's sake."

"Now Chief," I said with a brightness I certainly didn't feel, "calm down. She had no choice. The bastard demanded she run it—to get at me, I guess—or he would go to the other stations. Kate and I thought it would be better if we kept at least some control over it, hence Amanda. I thought she did a good job, don't you?"

"Hell *no*!"

I winced.

"This is going to get very ugly, Harry. I've already had a call from the damned sheriff. *Emoji?* He was laughing like a damned jackass. You said you wanted to keep the feds out of it, well, you just opened the damned door wide enough for them to drive a truck through. Good luck with that. Keep me friggin' posted." He turned and walked out, slamming the door behind him.

"Well," I said after a moment. "That went well."

Kate burst out laughing; Lonnie just sat there with that annoying, shit-eating grin on his face.

"Way to go, Harry," he said.

"It could have been a whole lot worse," Kate said. "So what now?"

"I guess we should turn Bobby Haskins loose, and his truck," I said. "It's not him, obviously."

"What about the other two?"

I shrugged. "Elkins? I don't see it. I don't think he's smart enough to come up with the Emoji thing. True, he has no alibi, and I think maybe he knew Jasmine, but I didn't push him on it. He also said he didn't know Dana. We could bring him in and grill him a little, I suppose. If he admits to knowing either of them…."

She nodded. "I think I agree. He's full of crap, but he's also borderline dumb. No. Let's put him aside, at least for now. What else do you have?"

"Lister?" I looked at her. She raised her eyebrows. "He thinks he's pretty smart," I continued, "but… well… his alibi is shot. He was either lying or he got the days mixed up; it's easy enough to do. He knew Jasmine. He didn't admit it, but I'm certain he knew her. Dana? I don't know yet. I didn't get to ask him, but I will."

"So," Lonnie said, "do we have a plan, or what?"

I thought for a minute, then said, "We need to find that teal truck, and its driver. He could be just a delivery boy driving our killer's red herring, but maybe he saw or knows something. Beyond that, we're back at square one, but with a whole heap of new problems thrown in." I shook my head. "Emoji, jeez. If the press are going to tag him with that label, we might as well climb on board too."

Kate shook her head, obviously not happy with the idea. By the look on Lonnie's face, however, he loved it.

"Okay," I said. "Here's what we need to do first. We need to find out a whole lot more about the first two victims: friends, boyfriends, etc. What were they doing in the weeks prior to their disappearances? I'd like to take a look at all three crimes scenes—not to see if you missed anything, just to get a feel for them. We need to get inside this… this… get inside his head." Even then I couldn't bring myself to use the moniker he seemed to have adopted for himself. One thing I was sure of, though: by the time this thing was done, I'd never want to see another emoji for the rest of my life.

"So," I continued, "Let's do this. Kate, you and I will go visit the sites. Lonnie, I want you to go see Joey Lister. There's something weird about him. He's smart enough to be… to do this thing. Grill him about his alibi. Find out if he was lying or just got the day wrong. I want to know if he knew Dana Walters or Jasmine Payne, or both. Find out if he has access to a pickup, no matter the color. Don't be gentle. Lean on him; bring him in if you want to; the inside of an interview room can work wonders. Don't arrest him; don't read him his rights. If he asks for an attorney, unless you think you have enough to charge him, turn him loose."

Oh yeah. Lonnie's the right person for this job.

"Now *that* sounds more like it," he said.

"Kate, I suggest you send Foote and Holtz back to UTC. Have them dig into the first victim, Dana Walters. Have them talk to her friends. I want to know if she had boyfriends or… was she… did she have a girlfriend? See if they can come up with anything that might link her to the other two or to any of our suspects. Have them try to trace her movements in the weeks before she disappeared. Yeah, I know," I said as her eyes widened, "it's been more than a year, but it's worth a try. There has to be something. We're just not seeing it. Tell them to take their time. It's important they don't leave anything out."

She nodded. "I'll set them to it." She made a call, spoke to Holtz and told him what she wanted. Lonnie hitched up his belt and headed for the door, still grinning. I shook my head. *My, how things have changed over the past three years. Time was, Lonnie and I couldn't stand the sight of each other. Now he's halfway likeable.*

"Okay Kate," I said, "are you driving or am I?"

"You are. You don't think I'd miss a chance at riding the Beast, do you? What about Jasmine Payne? I couldn't find anything then, but I didn't have the three stooges—suspects—then. I think we need to start over on that one too."

I nodded. "Do you have anyone to put on it?"

She thought for a moment, then shook her head.

"How about we put Bob on it?"

She nodded slowly.

I knew what she was thinking. She and Bob had until quite recently been in a somewhat torrid relationship. I'd always wondered what they had in common; they were the least likely pairing I could imagine. Anyway, they finally ended it, by mutual consent. They were still friends, but I could tell she had reservations, which was strange, because she and I had been an item for almost eight years and working with me didn't seem to bother her at all.

Finally, she said, "If you think… yes. That would work. I can't pay you for him though."

I smiled at her. "When did the PD ever pay me for anything? Let's drop by my offices and see if we can tear him loose for a couple of days."

Chapter 16

I had to smile when I walked into the office that afternoon.

"Where are Jacque and Bob Ryan?" I asked, smiling at them.

"What are you talkin' about?" Jacque asked, her hands on her hips. "We're both right here in front of you. Are you talking about our clothes?"

I nodded. "Very nice; very businesslike. I'm impressed."

Her great nest of black hair was piled high on top of her head and instead of the usual jeans and blouse, she was wearing a charcoal gray business suit with the skirt cut just above the knee. It was a look I'd never seen on her before, and it suited her; she looked spectacular… and so did Bob.

He looked… like he'd stepped right out of Humphrey Bogart movie. Yeah, I'd better explain. I've known Bob for years. He's my lead investigator, worked for me almost since the day I opened the agency. He's a big man, almost a year older than I am, six foot two and 240 pounds of mostly muscle, with a wry sense of humor and a fondness for a cut-down baseball bat. He's one of the toughest men I've ever met. He's been known to kill at the drop of a hat, and even drop that hat himself, if you know what I mean. You don't screw around with Bob. His voice is deep, almost a growl, menacing even when he's being nice, which he rarely ever is. I don't think I'd ever seen him in anything other than jeans.

So picture that man dressed in a white seersucker suit with a pale blue dress shirt, and you'll have an idea of how… different he looked. Oh, don't get me wrong. The suit was obviously expensive, and it fit him perfectly.

He looked at Kate, then at me, obviously self-conscious. Then he shrugged. "Well, you know. I thought, seeing as I'm now…. Seeing as Jacque decided to dress up…. Well, I figured I'd better try to look the part too." He pulled a face, tugged at the suit jacket. "Hell, man. It's frigging hot outside. They told me this would be cool." He laughed. It sounded like a rockslide. "Well, less warm."

I nodded. They really did look good, both of them.

"How's it going?" I asked. "I haven't heard from you since… well, since Monday."

"We're managing quite well, thank you," Jacque said. "We contacted everyone and most are happy enough, but there are a few holdouts who would like to talk to you. You want a list?"

"Eventually. But right now, no. We're buried in this case…."

"Yeah, we heard," Bob said, a huge smile on his face. "It's been on all the news stations, even the radio. WRIP had a field day with it. Emoji? What the hell is that about?"

"It's a long story," I said, "and I don't have time for now, but it's why we're here. Bob, I need a good investigator and, other than me—" I grinned at him "—that would be you. Can you turn yourself loose for a couple of days to do some prowling around for me?"

"Well. I'm working the Goodman case for Larry Spruce, but it's kinda hanging a little right now," he looked at Jacque. She shrugged and nodded.

"Yeah, a couple of days, then I'd need to—"

"Great," I said, handing him a copy of the Jasmine Payne file. "Two days, then. Let's go to my office and I'll explain what I need you to do."

Kate and I spent the next ten minutes going through the file with him. Bob's a quick study though, and there's no need, as they say, to teach your granny to suck eggs. Before we were halfway done he was telling us what was needed.

He promised he'd be on the job no later than five o'clock that evening, and we were back in the outer office and about to leave them to it when the thought hit me. I was so lucky to have these people.

On impulse, I grabbed hold of Jacque, wrapped both arms around her, and pulled her to me. She gasped with surprise.

"Thank you," I whispered in her ear. Then I let her go, turned to Bob and…. "Nooo," he said, backing away with his hands up, shaking his head.

I smiled at him and stuck out my hand. He took it. “Thanks, Bob, for everything. You too, Jacque.”

“Get the hell outta here,” he growled. “I’ll call you if I find anything.”

We got out.

“Oh, man,” Kate said as we walked to the car, “are you turning into some sort of wimp or what.”

“Nah, just grateful, is all. Those guys, all of them, are pretty special.... Come on, Kate. You know that.”

She nodded. “I do, especially Bob.”

“What happened between you two anyway?” I asked as she dropped into the passenger seat. “I thought you guys had a good thing going.”

“Yeah, I thought so too....” She shook her head. “I don’t want to talk about it, okay?”

Chapter 17

I drove north on I-75 toward Cleveland. It was one of those balmy, late summer afternoons when it was a joy just to be alive. The sky was a field of blue, dotted here and there with small white clouds. The temperature outside was hovering around eighty-four degrees; inside the car it was a comfortable seventy-one.

I took the Apison Pike Exit 9 and then turned left across the Interstate toward the VW plant. I drove on slowly until Kate sat up in her seat.

"Just there." She pointed to the right as we passed the end of the guardrails. "Slowly, slower—there, down there in the depression."

I pulled the Beast off the road onto a patch of bare ground, parked, and we climbed out and stood together looking down the slope into the depression. It wasn't steep, but it was maybe fifteen or twenty feet to the bottom, with trees and brush all around. The grass had been mowed recently though, and the walk down was easy enough.

"Over here, just beyond that rocky stretch." She pointed, and continued on across the grassy slope to the edge of the undergrowth. When they reached the rocks, she stood with her hands on her hips and nodded toward the spot.

In my mind's eye, I could see it: the body, naked, spread-eagled under a light covering of soggy brown leaves, her hair wet, tangled, spread out, strands lying on her face.

I took a couple of steps sideways and stared down at the spot. I blinked, and then blinked again. My head began to spin. I shook it. It cleared. I breathed deeply.

"Harry? *Harry?"*

I turned to look at her. "What?"

"Where were you? You were completely ignoring me."

"I didn't hear you. Sorry. Just give me a moment, okay?"

I backed up a couple of steps for a wider view of the scene, closed my eyes, breathed deeply, steadily, listening, waiting.... *What's that? The wind? No. There is no wind, not even a breeze. There it is again. Voices. A girl.... Someone crying... softly.*

I opened my eyes. I felt dizzy. I looked at the trees. They were out of focus. I rubbed my eyes, shook my head....

"Harry, dammit, you're scaring me. What is it?"

I shuddered, looked up at the scudding white clouds, took a deep breath, then turned to her. "Nothing. Nothing at all. Let's go. I've seen enough." I walked back up the slope to the car, and she followed, a few feet behind me.

The second scene was a little more than seven miles from the first. I parked in the Riverpark lot with Nickajack Dam to the right and the railway bridge to the left. The Chattanooga State Community College was just beyond, to the west of the bridge.

Kate took me to the spot where Jasmine Payne's body had been found. It was to the rear of one the great stanchions that supported the bridge. Hardly out of sight, it was easily seen from the parking lot.

Again, the grass had been mowed. I looked around, but there was nothing. It was just a pleasant spot twenty feet or so from the road and maybe thirty from the concrete path. The view across the river was lovely. The walk was busy: folks out running, power walking, or riding bikes.

We walked down to the riverbank, sat down on one of the wooden benches. We didn't talk. We just sat quietly for a few minutes, and then we went back to the car.

"So," she said. "Any thoughts?"

I shook my head. "Not a one."

It was a pleasant drive of just under a couple of miles to the third crime scene, where the body of Maggie Hart had been found, close to the C. B. Robinson Bridge. The tape had been removed and nothing remained to remind the walkers of the grisly find. The area was beautifully landscaped, the grass tightly manicured, and the tree, the tree where Maggie Hart was found sitting all alone, staring sightlessly out across the river was… just that, a tree.

I stood beside it, facing the river, closed my eyes, and breathed deeply, waiting, listening, but other than the birds singing, I heard nothing. For ten minutes I waited, my eyes closed, and then I gave up. There was nothing to see and no messages to receive.

I turned to Kate. She was seated a few yards away behind me at a picnic table. “Let’s go,” I said. “We still have a few minutes. We’ll go by my office and chat a little, then I’ll drop you off at the PD and head on home. Maybe something will come to me later.”

Sheesh, I sure as hell hope it doesn’t. At least, not like it did last night.

Chapter 18

I arrived home a little after six thirty to find that Amanda, wearing a red and white floral summer dress, was apparently ready to go out. That, for me at least, wasn't part of the plan. I'd been looking forward to a relaxing evening: a light dinner, a bottle of wine, maybe two, and a couple of hours poolside.

"Don't look at me like that," she said. "Your father called and asked us to join him and Rose for dinner."

"You should have called me. I'm in no mood for mingling with the.... Oh hell. You know what I'm talking about. After your segment today it's going to be a damned circus."

"It doesn't have to be. Besides, we haven't been out to dinner in weeks. I'm going stir crazy. Plus I told August we'd be there at seven thirty, so you have time to shower and change your clothes."

It was on the tip of my tongue to tell her go by herself, but I didn't. Instead I said nothing, and did as I was told.

The Country Club is a collective of old-world money and nouveau riche, an exclusive world where the so-called movers and shakers of our fair city gather together in the rarified air, ostensibly to play golf, make deals, drink and... well, to put it delicately, show off and play the field. Me? Yeah, I admit it's my world too, and useful to me, and especially my business, in more ways than I can count. I play golf most weekends, meet people and gather information. Everybody who is anybody is a member and on any given night the lounges and dining room are busy, some nights more so than others, which is why I was reluctant to go that night. But go I did.

Conversation between Amanda and me on the drive over that night was sparse. I had a lot on my mind, mostly Emoji. (I had reluctantly come to terms with the nickname.) Anyway, Amanda was driving that evening, which meant I could enjoy a drink. She slipped the Jaguar F Pace into a space close to the club steps, turned off the motor, and reached for the door handle. I put my hand on her arm.

"Hold on a minute," I said. "We need to talk."

She half turned toward me, tilted her head, and smiled. "Okay?"

"You did well today."

"The Emoji thing? Thank you."

"It's going to get unpleasant, isn't it?" I asked.

The smile slipped away. She nodded, slowly.

"Amanda, I need you to…. Now hold on." She was shaking her head. "Let me finish. I told you we have a leak at the PD. I need to know who it is. Did you talk to him or her?"

"No, Harry. I didn't."

Again she reached for the door handle, and again I stopped her.

"Look, I understand, but this is important. We're dealing with a serial murderer and leaked information could seriously screw things up. If you know who it is, you need to tell me."

"I don't know who it is…. And even if I did, I wouldn't… I couldn't tell you. I'm sorry, Harry."

I sighed, laid my head on the headrest, and stared up at… nothing.

"Okay," I said finally. "I'll make sure you get the exclusive. In return, I want you to handle the newscasts and I want you keep me in the loop; you get a call, an e-mail, a text, whatever, you call me, run it by me…. No, hold on. I don't want to censor you. And I won't. I just need advance warning of what I'm up against. Can we agree on that?"

She nodded slowly, thinking. "With some rules, yes."

"Okay, good, we can talk about that later. What I'd like to know now is, can we keep it exclusive to Channel 7?"

"I doubt it. If you *do* have a leak at the PD, the other outlets will be willing to pay and…." She looked at me, slowly shaking her head. "If the nationals get hold of it…."

"Friggin' hell," I muttered. "Not again. Oh hell. I need a drink in the worst way. Let's go inside."

August was at the bar, surrounded by friends, as always. Rose, bless her, was seated at my favorite table in the huge bay window overlooking the river and the ninth green; she was sipping a glass of white wine. I slid into the seat beside her, and Amanda sat next to me.

"He left you all alone," I said, giving her a peck on the cheek. "Can't understand why. You *rook* marvelous." It was a poor impersonation, but it made her smile.

"Oh you know how he is," she said. "He's just making the rounds. He'll join us soon."

She took my hand in both of hers. "How is it going Harry, Amanda?" She looked across me at Amanda.

"This… this Emoji thing, you mean?" I asked.

She nodded.

"The storm's gathering, I think, but I'll get through it. I always do. Don't we, Amanda?"

Amanda nodded.

"How are *you*, Amanda? Everything's okay, the baby an' all?"

"Oh yes. No morning sickness yet. I'm eating like a hog at meals and snacking on anything and everything in between. Would you believe I've already put on ten pounds?"

"*No*," I said forcefully. "I wouldn't."

"Shopping then," Rose said delightedly. "Baby clothes… and clothes—lovely dresses—for you. Oh, we're going to have fun. Ah… New York. We'll go to New York…."

"The hell you will," August said loudly, as he slipped into the seat beside her. "Harry my boy," he boomed. "What the hell have you gotten yourself mixed up in this time? Emoji? What the hell is that? I've been fielding questions ever since we arrived. They say we have a serial killer on the loose. What say you?"

"I say shut the hell up about it. I came here for a nice evening, a nicer dinner, and an even nicer drink or two, maybe even three or four." I sighed. "Dad, you know I can't talk about it, and I wouldn't if I could. So let's change the subject. How are you? And why did you leave Rose here all by herself?"

"Can't talk about it? Won't?" He shrugged. "I understand. Yes, let's change it. I didn't leave her. I just went to get a drink and I got… well, Harry. You know how it is. And speaking of drinks, what will you have? Amanda?"

"Laphroaig," I said. "A big one."

"I'll get them," Amanda said. "You might get lost again." She smiled at him.

"Good girl," he said. "Put 'em on my tab, and get me another one while you're at it, Bombay Sapphire with a splash of tonic, a big one, and get one for Rose too."

She slipped out of the seat and walked to the bar. I watched her go and, for the umpteenth time, I wondered how I'd gotten so lucky.

She returned just a couple of moments later. "Charles will bring the drinks."

And Charles did. He set the tray down and handed Amanda what looked like a glass of red wine, though the shape of the glass was all wrong.

"Er… what are you…."

"What am I drinking?" she interrupted me, eyebrows raised. "Cranberry juice, of course."

"And on that sour note," August said. "I suggest we order."

He looked around, waved down one of the waiters, and we ordered. It was right about then, when we were easing back, talking quietly amongst ourselves and waiting for our food to arrive, that I noticed someone staring at me. As soon as he saw that I'd seen him, he looked quickly away. At first I didn't think much of it, but then I caught him doing it again. And again, he looked quickly away. So then I was watching him, and it happened several more times.

"What are you doing?" Amanda asked, nudging me. "Rose was asking a question."

"Sorry, I'm sorry…. August, who is that man over there? The group of four, the guy on the right in the blue and white striped shirt."

August turned, looked at him, then turned back again. "That's Dr. Greenwood; David Greenwood. Nice guy. Head in the clouds, maybe, but friendly enough. Why?"

Greenwood? That name sounds familiar.

"I've caught him staring at me a few times."

"Hah," August laughed. "I wonder why. Your face has been all over Channel 7, lunchtime and this evening. You're famous, Harry… or should that be infamous?"

I shrugged and pulled a face. "Is he a member? If he is, how come I don't know him?"

"Yes he's a member. Has been for as long as I can remember, and his father before him. He's not here often. Doesn't play golf. Can you believe that?"

"Hah. He's a doctor, you say? What sort of doctor?"

"He's a clinical psychologist. Wears two hats. Has a small, one-man practice on Vine Street, I believe. Specializes in corporate work, mental health of employees and the like. He also teaches psychology at UTC."

So that's it. That's how I know the name.

Now I stared at him unabashedly. He was a good-looking man, trim and fit, perhaps five foot nine but no more than that. He was in his early forties, perhaps; his hair showed no gray that I could see, but it was receding slightly. He sat very erect, his back straight, eating in the English manner—fork upside down in his left hand, knife in his right, forefinger on top.

What's his interest in me, I wonder?

I squeezed Amanda's hand under the table, then said, "Tell me about him, Dad."

August shrugged, put down his fork, wiped his mouth on his napkin, and said, "There's not much to tell. His family is quite well off, old money… well, his wife's family is; he's English, a naturalized citizen, I believe. They're in the oil business. No, not oil wells, a distributorship, that's it. They own a number of One Stop convenience stores in and around the city and the county. They have a small oil depot off Jersey Pike from which they supply only their own stores with gas.

"I don't know where he went to school. Somewhere in England—Oxford or Cambridge, most likely. He's been on Vine Street for years, and at the university. I have a drink with him now and again, play a little poker, but I don't know him that well. Uh oh, he's coming over here."

He was, and the first thing I noticed about him was the walk: he walked quickly, took very small steps. If you've ever watched the Hercule Poirot movies, you'll know exactly what I mean.

"Please," he said when he reached us. "Don't get up. I don't mean to intrude, August, but I was watching Channel 7 News at lunchtime—I do so love to watch you, Mrs. Starke—and, well, you know, all that stuff; it's… it's interesting to say the least. That being said, August, I was wondering if you might introduce me to your son. I have a professional interest, you see, in the workings of the criminal mind—oh, I'm terribly sorry. I didn't mean that you have a criminal mind, Mr. Starke."

I didn't answer. I smiled up at him and rose to my feet. I wasn't quite sure how to take what he'd just said. I had the distinct feeling that he had a hidden agenda.

"Yes, of course," August said, and he stood too.

"Harry, Amanda. This is Dr. David Greenwood. I'm surprised you don't already know each other, you both being members here."

Greenwood smiled, widely, showed his teeth, ignored August and Rose, walked around the table, and leaned over Amanda, his hand extended for me to shake. She leaned back, away from him, and I took it. His grip was… not exactly limp, but it wasn't firm either.

"Mr. Starke," he gushed. "I'm *so* pleased to meet you. I've heard *so* much about you, but then, haven't we all?" He laughed, no, he brayed like a damned donkey, and looked around the table, beaming. "This case you're working on. I find it intriguing. One isn't often afforded the opportunity to observe something like that firsthand. I wonder," he said, "if one of these days, when you have nothing better to do, you might spare me a few moments of your time. I'd absolutely *love* to talk to you. It would be, I'm sure, a valuable learning experience… perhaps for both of us." That last was said with a somewhat sardonic smile.

What the hell did he mean by that? Oh yeah, he's English, and upper class too, judging by that accent.

There was something about the look on his face that I didn't quite get. The slight tilt of the head. His eyes, half narrowed, bored into mine, and then there was the smile. His lips were smiling, but his eyes weren't. *Is he mocking me?*

I stared at him. I know I had a stupid smile on my face, because afterward Amanda couldn't wait to tell me so. Anyway, I was so taken aback, I didn't know what to say.

"Well… yes… I suppose we could get together, sometime. Why don't you give my PA… sorry, my partner, Jacque Hale, a call? Maybe we can set something up."

"Excellent. Excellent. I'll do that. I have your number." The eyes glinted. Was it the lighting, or…?

He has my number? I could take that two ways.

"Now," he said briskly. "I mustn't disturb you good people any further. It was *so* nice to finally meet you both. Enjoy the rest of your evening."

And he turned and minced—yes, minced—away, back to his table.

He has my number? I sure as hell don't have his.

"Wow," Amanda said, staring after him. "What was that about?"

"I'm not sure," I replied, "but I have a feeling I'll soon find out. That man has an agenda."

And I was sure he did, but I soon forgot about him. My dad has a way of doing that to you, and we did indeed enjoy the rest of the evening.

We arrived home that night tired and ready to sleep, or at least Amanda was. Me? Not so much. I poured myself a drink and went out to the pool, to the patio, and sat down, ostensibly to think. In reality, I was reluctant to go to bed. I was half expecting visitors.

I shouldn't have worried. When I finally made it to bed I slept the sleep of the dead, dreamless and deep.

Chapter 19

It was just after eight thirty when I walked into Kate's office that next morning, and I was feeling pretty good. For the first time in what seemed like weeks, although really it was only days, I'd slept the night through. The only thing that woke me up was my alarm clock.

Kate, on the other hand, didn't look well at all. Her face was pale, lips drawn.

"Thank God you're here," she said. "There's another one."

"Another what? A body?"

"No. Another student has been reported missing. Chloe Sandoval, twenty-two years old. She was reported missing early this morning, at 12:05, by her mother. They live in Hixson, on Carter Drive."

I sat down across from her. "*Damn*!" I shook my head. "It's too soon, Kate. We only found the last one five days ago. Are we sure it's connected?"

"No, not yet. The mother said Chloe left the house around ten last night to go to Food City, on Hixson Pike, for some ice cream. When she didn't return, her mother went looking for her and found her car in the Food City parking lot. She tried calling her but the girl's phone went straight to voicemail. Mike Willis has the security camera footage from the store and is going through it right now."

I got to my feet. "Let's go see what he's found. Maybe we'll get lucky."

We did get lucky—and we didn't. There was good footage of Chloe's Honda, and of Chloe going into the store, and no sooner had she exited her car and walked away, than a second vehicle, a late model silver Nissan Rogue, pulled up alongside the Honda, its passenger side next to it. When Chloe returned she would have to pass between the two cars to regain access to hers.

We watched as she returned to her car. She was carrying a single grocery bag—the ice cream, I presumed.

She passed between the two cars, turned to open her door, stopped, turned again to face the passenger window of the Rogue and leaned forward. Even at that angle it was easy to see that she was smiling. She talked, she listened, she smiled, she shook her head, then shrugged, nodded, opened the Nissan's door, and got in. No sooner had she done so, even before the door closed, the Nissan rocketed away; the door slamming shut under the force of the acceleration. Without slowing, it swerved out of the parking lot onto Hixson Pike heading north, fast.

Willis stopped the video. Leaned back in his seat. Even though I knew he'd seen it before, at least once, I could tell he was stunned by what we'd just seen. We'd just watched Chloe Sandoval being abducted.

“There’s more,” Willis said. “I got the license plate. I had to enhance it some, but you’re not going to believe this.”

He tapped the keyboard, clicked the mouse, and the screen filled with a close up of the rear of the Nissan.

I was dumbfounded. “Son of a bitch.”

“Oh. My. God,” Kate said.

“Yeah,” Mike said. “That and more. Here’s a copy for you. Enjoy.” He handed Kate a thumb drive. “Now, if you don’t mind. I have things to do. If you need me….”

***

“What do you think?” Kate asked, turning the monitor slightly so Lonnie and I could get a better look.

“Are you friggin’ serious?” Lonnie asked.

Together we stared at the image of the license plate. A sheet of white paper had been taped over it and there, dead center, was the emoji, the same one we’d received two days ago that seemed to be telling us, *Bring it on.*

I shook my head. “Run the footage, Kate. Maybe we’ll catch something, though I doubt it. This is one smart son of a bitch. He knew about those security cameras and he didn’t care.”

We ran the footage three times—there were only eleven minutes of it—and we learned exactly nothing.

Oh, she knew the driver, and she knew him well. Obviously she felt comfortable enough to enter his car; what for, there was no clue. From the way the Nissan screeched away, it seemed unlikely it was just to talk. I had a feeling we'd never know. What we *did* know was that Emoji had struck again.

"Kate, Lonnie," I said. "Only we three and Mike Willis know about the license plate. We need to keep it that way."

They both nodded.

We all leaned back in our chairs and regarded one another, thinking, no one saying a word, and then, one after another, our cell phones chirped, beeped, and in my case, barked like a dog. We all had received text messages.

The sender was listed as unknown, but I had a feeling I knew who it was. Mine was an image. I opened it. It was a photo of the emoji: *Bring it on*, only this time it was a little different. There was a large black number three inscribed just below the image.

"You get the same?" I asked holding the phone up for them to see.

"Yeah," Lonnie said.

Kate nodded. "What does it mean?"

"I don't know, but I can—"

My phone barked again; another text.

Same rules as before, Starke. Amanda handles the coverage. If she doesn't, and if it's not on the early newscast today, I'll go to the other outlets. She's still alive. You have three days.

"Oh jeez," I sighed. "This is turning into a nightmare. Three days for what?"

"To find her," Lonnie said grimly. "Before he kills her."

I had a hollow feeling in my gut that he was right, but how were we going to do that?

"You talked to Joey Lister, right?" I asked him.

"Yeah, like you said. I dragged his ass in here. I took him apart. He couldn't explain about the mix up in the days when he supposed to have been at the Bonefish. He said he must have made a mistake. I dunno, Harry. I gave it my best shot. He came close to tears one time, said that all of the evenings on campus are the same and that he couldn't tell one from another. When I'd finished with him I went to see the Lockerby girl. She was with him all right, but on Tuesday, not Wednesday."

"What about Dana Walters and Jasmine Payne? Did he know either or both of them?"

"He admitted to knowing Jasmine. Said he'd asked her out a couple of times, but she'd turned him down. Dana Walters?" He shrugged. "Claims he'd heard of her but had never met her. I couldn't get anything more from him."

"Lonnie," I said. "Lister drives a 2015 silver Nissan Rogue, and now I have to wonder if he knew Chloe. We need to find out if he has an alibi for between nine thirty and ten thirty last night."

"I'll go haul his ass back in here and give him another going over. LT," he said to Kate, "I gotta tell you, I don't believe a word he's said so far. I think it's him. I think we should throw his ass in jail. We have probable cause. The son of a bitch lied to us about knowing Jasmine *and* about where he was the night Maggie Hart disappeared. He has no alibi for the night Jasmine went missing. And he has the right make and model vehicle. We can hold him without charging him for forty-eight hours."

Kate looked at me. I shook my head. "He drives a Rogue, Lonnie. But as far as we know, he doesn't have a truck."

"Yeah, but, we know for sure that this Chloe kid was abducted in a Nissan…."

"You're right, Lonnie, but…. Well, go get him. We'll decide whether or not to hold him later."

He nodded, and left us alone.

I looked at Kate. "The Nissan is a game changer, Kate. What happened to the truck?"

She just closed her eyes and shook her head. I knew just how she felt.

"What about these texts?" she asked, looking down at her iPhone. "Can we trace them, d'you think?"

"We can try, but I doubt it. 'Number Unknown.' That means it's probably a burner, and probably already in a dumpster somewhere."

My phone rang in my hand. I flipped the screen and put it to my ear. "Hey, sweetheart," I said. "You got one too, I guess?"

She had, along with the same message I'd received. I was still talking to her when the door burst open and Chief Johnston stormed in, his iPhone in his hand.

"I'll call you right back," I told Amanda, and disconnected.

"For Christ's sake, people," he growled. "This shit has hit every smart phone and most of the computers in the damned building, and we have another abduction. I've seen that damned license plate. This son of a bitch is playing with you, Harry."

"Well," I said, shaking my head, "so much for us trying to keep it to ourselves. Our leaker will have it on the networks before we do."

"Have you made any progress at all?" Johnston asked. "Do you have a suspect?"

We could have lied to him, told him that we did have a suspect, Joey Lister, but I had a feeling it wasn't him. This Emoji thing, especially the broadcasted texts, was way out of his league.

"No, Chief. We have nothing concrete. Not yet."

"Shit," he said under his breath. "Shit, shit, shit." He looked at me. "You've got to get this bastard, Harry, and soon. If not… I'm going to have to ask the FBI for help. With this new kid missing, and this threat hanging in the air, I should do it now."

"You're right," I said. "You should, and yes, you should do it right now."

Kate looked sharply at me.

I shrugged. "Chief, this thing is escalating. We have to do everything we can to find the kid before he kills her. Call them and ask them for aid. It's the right thing to do."

He nodded, looked at me and then at Kate, then turned away and left us alone again.

I called Amanda. "Hey," I said. "You want to know how to handle the texts, right? Same as before. A short piece. A few sentences, no more. Tell them about the latest abduction—" I heard her gasp. "Oh hell, you didn't know, did you? Well now you do. Her name is Chloe Sandoval. She's twenty-two, lives in Hixson, and is a student at UTC. *Do not* release her name or where she lives. That family has enough on their hands without a horde of reporters to deal with. Just say something like, 'The police are withholding details, yada, yada, yada.' But I don't have to tell you how to do your job. Just do what you need to do, and run it by me and Kate before you go on air, please."

She told me to give her an hour and she'd have something ready. Then she paused. It was a long pause. Harry…" she said eventually. "Oh you're going to be pissed. Someone sent us a copy of an image of a car license plate…."

"Holy *Mary* mother of *God*," I shouted down the phone, cutting her off.

I looked at Kate. Her eyes were wide. *What?* she mouthed.

I shook my head. "Sorry, Amanda."

"It's okay. It was just the plate. We couldn't tell the make and model of the car."

"Oh hell. How the hell…? Oh, dear Jesus. Shit's gonna hit the fan. Was there a message with it?"

"Yeah. 'Run it or else.' That was all. Harry, I have to run it. I have no choice. They're preparing it as we speak. I'll be on air with an update at noon, and I'll record two extended pieces, different pieces, one to run at six, the other at eleven. I'll fax the scripts over for you to read. Don't expect to make any big changes, though." She paused. "Look, I gotta go. I'll talk to you this afternoon, okay?" And then she disconnected, leaving me staring soullessly at the phone.

Kate's desk phone rang. She picked it up, listened, nodded, then said, "Okay. Yes. Yes. I will, I'll let him know," and put the handset back in its cradle.

"Well," she said, leaning back in her chair. "It might not be as bad as we thought. Johnston didn't call in the FBI. He compromised and called Director

Condon at the TBI. Your buddies from Knoxville will be here tomorrow morning. In the meantime, I have to get information packages prepared for them, and you need to try to stop any further damage, and work with Amanda." She paused. "And one more thing. How the hell did he get that security footage?"

"Maybe he didn't," I said. "Maybe he simply snapped a photo, a close up, of the plate with his phone. Then forwarded it to Channel 7."

But did he?

I wondered.

Chapter 20

The Tennessee Bureau of Investigation's finest arrived at eight thirty in the morning: Special Agents Gordon Caster and Sergio Mendez, plus half a dozen of their staff.

They hadn't changed much over the year that had passed since I'd called them in to help with the murder of Chief Johnston's daughter, Emily. That was when I'd first met them. We'd grown to be… not exactly friends. I didn't trust either one of them, and they certainly didn't trust me. No, they hadn't changed a bit. They still were what they were, special agents in every sense of the words.

They were an impressive, though incongruous pair. Caster might well have been FBI; he had it stamped all over him, from the dark gray suit to the heavy black shoes. He was tall, extremely fit, maybe forty years old—I'd never asked him—quiet, dignified, all business. Mendez was smaller by a couple of inches, and a little heavier. He was dressed, as always, in blue jeans, a matching denim shirt, open at the neck, cowboy boots, and a tan leather jacket.

We assembled in the conference room at the Police Services Center.

Kate and the chief had already met the pair several times, but introductions had to be made to

Lonnie and the other detectives involved in the case. Coffee was served, and then Chief Johnston took a seat at the head of the table, Kate on his right and me on the left.

Kate and I spent the next two hours bringing the TBI guys up to date on what we knew so far—at least, as much as we were sure we knew. Me? I had an idea of my own slowly building inside my head and that, I decided, I'd keep to myself. I wouldn't even tell Kate and Amanda until I was sure I had it right.

Now, you should know that the TBI are very much in tune with the FBI, especially in the way they like to work. They look on local law enforcement as a poor relative, more of a hindrance than help, and Castor and Pollux—okay, Caster and Mendez—were no different. They sucked Kate and I dry—or they tried to. They took over a suite of three offices and the conference room and then, for all intents and purposes, they turned their backs and ignored us, which was just fine with me.

Kate and I returned to her office and the incident room, fully expecting to never hear from the elite team of investigators ever again. Unfortunately, that was not to be the case. Barely had we sat down than there was a knock at the door, and a young TBI officer stuck her head in.

"Um, hi, I'm sorry to… well, it seems I'm going to be your liaison with the TBI. I'm supposed to join your group, keep an… whoops, that would be… um, to ensure and facilitate the free transfer of information between our two departments. My name is Agent Holly Atkins."

I almost laughed at her. "Well, Holly Atkins," I said, as pleasantly as I could. "You can return from whence you came and tell Special Agent Caster that we don't need a liaison, or his help, or yours, and we certainly don't need his spy running back and forth screwing up the good order and smooth running of our own investigation. And it is still our investigation. Now, away you go, and don't come back."

And she left.

"Do you think that was a good idea, Harry?" Kate asked. "Antagonizing those who have no equals?"

I did laugh at that one. "Eh, who the hell cares? What are they going to do? Shut us down? I don't think so. This is our—your patch; they're invited guests, and only here on sufferance. Now, let's forget about them and get back to work."

"But what if they screw up what we're doing? Treading on toes we don't want trodden on?"

"Like who?"

"Well, Amanda for one."

"Now that really is funny. She's been dealing with the likes of them for almost as long as we have, but a whole lot more often. She can handle herself, and the TBI. Hell, Kate. Don't you remember how she used to treat me, before she and I…? I'll call her and let her know what's going on. Now, can we get to work?"

We could, but before we did, I called Amanda and warned her that she'd probably be getting a visit from the TBI, and to be careful what she told them.

She laughed and told me not to worry. I hung up with the distinct impression that she'd get more out the dynamic duo than they would get out of her.

"Did Stop and Go come up with anything new?" I asked Kate. The short answer was no.

Detectives Foote and Holtz had spent the past two days on and around the UT campus, interviewing anyone and everyone who might have known the three girls, anyone who might have spotted something, anything… and they'd come up with nothing, which didn't surprise me, because as I said, I had an idea of my own brewing.

Around eleven thirty, Kate received a call from Booking. Lonnie had dragged Joey Lister in in chains—well, handcuffs—which Lister's public defender promptly had him remove, and then he,

Lonnie, settled in to grill the poor bastard. I didn't want any part of it; I really didn't think Lister was smart enough for it, for one thing, and he didn't have a pickup for a second, but what the hell. You never know.

In the meantime, I had a call to make. I needed to talk to Maggie Hart's sister Christie, and I didn't need an audience.

***

I went outside to my car, climbed in—no, I dropped in—sank deep into the leather, and tapped in the number.

I had to do this right. I was going fishing. I needed to know if Maggie knew Professor David Greenwood, but I didn't want to put ideas in Christie's head.

"Christie? This is Harry Starke. Listen. I need a little help. I've run out of names. I'm trying to come up with a list of people we can talk to that might be able to shed some light on this thing. We've talked to all her friends, including Charlie Elkins, Bobby Haskins, and Joey Lister, and we got very little. So, Christie, can you think of anyone we might have missed? She was an art major, right?"

"Yes, she was. Have you talked to Lacy Stewart or Mike Hammond? They're both art majors. Not close friends of hers, but she knew them both well.... What about Professor Booth? Have you spoken to her? She probably knew her better than anyone in the department."

"Hmmm, that's an idea."

Kate had already spoken to the woman. She'd been no help at all, but like I said, I was fishing.

"Anyone else? Any other members of the faculty that might be able to help?" I held my breath.

"No… I don't think so."

Damn. This is like pulling teeth.

I took a deep breath and dived right in.

"Hmmm," I said. "How about you? How about your professors? D'you think any of them might have seen anything? How about Doug Wiggins? Would it be worth my while talking to him, d'you think?" I took another deep breath and said, "Or Professor Greenwood?"

"I… I don't know." She hesitated. "They both knew her, through me of course, so she did know both of them casually. Both of them had stopped for a cup of coffee with us at Starbucks a couple times. You know the kind of thing I'm talking about. She liked to talk to them. She was curious, you know, but I don't see how talking to them… but, sure, why not."

So they both knew her, and she knew them. I wonder….

I thanked her and said goodbye, then sat there for a moment, thinking. Then I called Bob. He was at the office.

"Hey," I said. "I haven't heard from you. Did you find anything?"

"I'm not done yet. I said I'd call you when I was."

"I know, but something's come up. Jasmine was a psychology major. Her professor was Dr. David Greenwood, so we know they knew each other. What I need to know is if they knew each other socially. I also need you to find out how well she knew Douglas Wiggins. I know she took classes with him too. But be careful. I don't want either of them—the two professors, I mean—to know we're asking questions about them."

"Are they suspects, Harry?"

"At this point, no...."

"Hah, so you say. Okay. Consider it done. Like I said, I'll call you. Keep the faith, Harry." He disconnected.

We spent the rest of the day and most of the next spinning our wheels, going over the same ground again and again to no avail. The TBI spent the two days re-interviewing everyone, including Elkins and Haskins; Joey Lister, still in custody, was eventually handed over to Caster and his crew; they had no better luck with him than Lonnie had and eventually, just as the forty-eight-hour deadline was approaching, we turned him loose.

Amanda did her thing at noon, and again at six and eleven. The result was a flood of calls from just about every nut in Hamilton County and beyond. But that wasn't all. Every TV and radio station from Chattanooga to Atlanta to Knoxville and Nashville had gotten in on the act. The local hotels were at capacity, and I figured it would be only a matter of time before the nationals arrived, which they did on the morning of September twelfth.

Because on the morning of the eleventh, Emoji struck again. At precisely nine o'clock, virtually every cell phone and e-mail account received another message from the killer: another *bring it on* graphic. This time it was inscribed with the number two. Two days left? And on the morning of September twelfth, another. This time the number was one.

And that night, for the first time three days, I had the dream again.

It was four o'clock in the morning when I awoke with jerk, sweating profusely. This time there were four of them. Three I knew well, and a new one, Chloe Sandoval. Like before, they had on white shifts, but this time they were all holding hands. They stood beside the bed, looking down at me reprovingly. Chloe was crying; tears were rolling down her cheeks.

She was dead. I knew it. I'd let her down… I'd let them all down…. I tried to speak to them, but the words wouldn't come. The girls all huddled together. And then they were gone. I rubbed my eyes, looked around the darkened room. The silence was palpable; I could almost touch it. Thankfully, though, the beast of my childhood was absent. I looked at Amanda. She was sleeping soundlessly.

I slipped out of bed as quietly as I could, then went outside and dived into the pool, hoping the cold water would wash away what I knew to be true. It didn't.

I went back into the house, retrieved my phone, and called Kate.

"Harry," she mumbled, still half asleep. "What the hell? It's only four thirty…."

"I know, but it's about Chloe. She's dead, Kate."

Chapter 21

"What?" Kate said. Her voice was sharp, now; suddenly she sounded completely awake. "What do you mean, she's dead? How do you know?"

"Trust me. I know. I'll pick you up in thirty minutes. Call Guest and the others. Have 'em go to the Riverwalk. Have them spread out, go to different spots. You and I will go to the north end, where Maggie was found. The son of a bitch will want to dump her body. Maybe we can catch him in the act."

"Harry, the Riverwalk is more than ten miles, and we'll be doing this in the dark."

"You think I don't know that? Look, we don't have time for this. Thirty minutes. Be ready."

***

It was just after six o'clock that morning—just after first light—when we found her. She was seated at a picnic table close to the footbridge over South Chickamauga Creek, at a popular spot known as Riverpoint. She was seated with her back to the concrete path, her head on her arms, which were folded on top of the table. If I hadn't known better, I'd have thought she was asleep. Kate spotted her as I drove slowly toward the circular turnaround.

"Look." She pointed. "There."

My heart sank. Somehow, I knew immediately that it was her, and that we were too late. We'd missed him.

I parked the car in one of the spaces just north of the picnic table twenty or so yards from the scene, and then we walked back. Not wanting to contaminate the site, we halted on the concrete path some thirty feet behind her.

"You'd better go check for life signs, Kate," I said sadly. "You won't find any, but it's protocol. It has to be done. I'll call it in."

I watched her as I made the call. She touched the girl's neck, held the contact for a moment, then turned and shook her head.

I sighed, completed the call, and then called Lonnie and told him where we were; Kate called Foote and Holtz. Then, together, we sat glumly on one of the park benches and waited.

In the distance we heard the sirens coming closer.

It was almost seven thirty when Doc Sheddon arrived. By then a whole section of the Walk had been cordoned off; Mike Willis and his crew had arrived thirty minutes earlier, but were waiting for the medical examiner before they began.

"Harry, Harry, Harry," Sheddon said, shaking his head as he ambled toward us, loaded down with the huge black bag he always brought to crime scenes. "What were you doing out here at this ungodly hour? Don't you ever sleep? No, I don't suppose you do. Damned vampire, you are. Hey, Kate. You too, I see. So. Let's go take a look, shall we? Suit up, please."

We grabbed Tyvek suits, booties, head covers, masks, and latex gloves from one of the boxes Mike Willis had dumped on the road and Kate, Lonnie, Doc Sheddon and I all "suited up."

He led the way, ducking under the tape and hauling the black bag with him, then waddled across the grass to the picnic table.

He stood back. We stood further back, watching, waiting.

We watched him put the bag down and walk slowly around the table, his chin on his chest, peering over the top of his signature half-moon glasses. His gloved hands hung loosely by his sides.

We watched him stop and kneel on the bench beside her, lift her head slightly, lean in close, lower it again, then step back off the bench and to her right side. He reached out, lifted her hand, spread the fingers, stared at them, turned the hand over, rubbed his thumb over the palm, nodded, lifted the hand to his nose, sniffed, and then put it back on the table.

Gently, he squeezed the bicep, and then he pinched the flesh on her right thigh, all the time mumbling to quietly to himself.

He stepped back, around the body to the left side, crouched, slipped a finger under the hem of the leg of her shorts and pulled it higher up her thigh. He ran a finger along the underside of her thigh, pinched again, nodded, stood, stepped back, and then turned and walked to where we were standing.

"All right, then," he said, "I can't do much more here. She was strangled. Possibly more than once. Whether or not strangulation was the cause of death, I can't say with any certainty until I've done the post. She hasn't been out here long. I'd say she's been dead between twenty and twenty-four hours. The arms, head, and neck are free from rigor, though the thighs are still a little stiff, so I'd say closer to twenty-four. She was posed, of course. I think she was placed in a chair soon after death with her arms hanging at her sides; either that or she died sitting upright in one. Lividity is set. I can't see her buttocks, but it's visible in the back of her thighs, hands, and fingers, and her ankles and feet."

"You said she hasn't been there long," I said. "How long?"

He tilted his head and squinted at me, blinking like an owl. "An hour and a half. Maybe a little less."

"Jesus," Kate whispered. "We must have missed him by minutes."

"Would she have been limp enough for him to pose her like that?" I asked, nodding toward the corpse.

"Oh yes. Easy to carry, too. She can't weigh much more than a hundred pounds."

"How quickly can you do the post?" I asked.

"Not today! I already have one on the table and another one waiting. I'll do it first thing tomorrow morning. Will you two attend?"

"I'll have to," Kate said.

Doc looked at me next, but I put my hands up.

"Not only no, but hell no. I told you; I'm done with all that. Never again."

"Well. There's nothing more I can do here. I'll have the body removed and you can turn the scene over to Mick Willis…." He looked at me. "You need to be there, Harry."

I didn't answer, and I wouldn't. Watching him carve up another kid was more than I could stomach.

I watched as he closed up his bag. When he was done he looked sideways up at me, shook his head slightly, then nodded, "You're right, Harry, and I've just about had enough of it too; I need to quit this life. The one I have to do this morning—" he shook his head again "—a little boy, seven years old, throat cut, raped: they found him a dumpster. Now I have to violate him even further. Makes me wonder if there is a God."

He stood, picked up the bag, and said, "See you tomorrow, Kate. Harry, don't lose hope, my friend." And with that he ambled slowly away, head down, a very sad old man. I knew exactly how he felt.

I told Kate goodbye, that I'd see her later in the day, and went home to try to catch up on some sleep. I arrived there a little after eight o'clock, after Amanda had already left for work. I felt like shit, and I didn't think I'd ever get over it, but I did. By two that afternoon I was back in my own office, the door firmly closed, going through the files, looking for… something… anything, but I found nothing of substance, other than the one name that, for some reason, kept bugging me.

Dr. David Greenwood.

I spoke to Kate briefly on the phone, and to Bob in person, and then I headed back up the mountain. By the time Amanda arrived at just after five that afternoon, I was there waiting for her.

She went straight to the TV and turned it to Channel 7 and the six o'clock news, which had been recorded earlier.

She, as usual, looked stunning in a pale blue sleeveless dress. I turned to look at her. She was still wearing it.

"You're not going to like this," she said, turning up the sound.

I looked at the screen as she began to speak.

"The body of Chloe Sandoval, who was abducted from the Food City parking lot on Hixson Pike four days ago, was discovered early this morning by detectives from the Chattanooga Police department. The body was found seated at a picnic table on the Riverwalk.

"A source close to the investigation stated that Detective Lieutenant Catherine Gazzara is convinced that it's the work of the serial killer they are calling Emoji." She paused for a moment, stared into the camera, and then continued. "Emoji, because this and other local stations have twice received copies of the graphic you see in the top right corner of your screen.

"Working on a tip from an anonymous source, detectives began searching the entire length of the Tennessee Riverpark early this morning. The park follows the Tennessee River from Chickamauga Dam to Ross's Landing, a distance of approximately ten miles. The body was discovered close to the pedestrian bridge that spans South Chickamauga Creek. If Chloe Sandoval is indeed the victim of Emoji, she would be the fourth victim in the last twelve months. That's all the details we have for now. Channel 7 News will bring you breaking news on the Emoji case as it happens."

The camera switched to her co-anchor.

"Where did you get all that?" I asked quietly, already knowing the answer.

"You know better than to ask me that, Harry."

"Yeah, I do, and I friggin' hate it. It's someone at the PD, right? Leaking the stuff to the other stations?"

She gave me the evil eye, said nothing.

"Well, at least you kept my name out of it. Thank you."

"Yes, I did, didn't I? I shouldn't have, because the other stations didn't. You're about to become a celebrity again."

"Oh hell," I said. "That, I could do without."

Chapter 22

The following morning I rose early and went for my usual run along East Brow almost to Covenant College and then back. I had a light breakfast with Amanda and then headed in to my office.

I arrived to find the entrance to the lot blocked by two remote TV broadcast vans. The reporters and camera operators, already armed with mikes and cameras, were waiting for me.

I rolled down my window. A mike and camera were immediately stuck in my face.

"Mr. Starke," the woman holding the mike said, "What can you tell us about Emoji and Chloe Sandoval?"

I stuck my hand over the camera lens and said, "No comment. Now get that van away from my gate or I'll have it towed."

Reluctantly, they backed away, the camera still running. I rolled up my window and waited for the van to be moved, then I clicked the button and the gate rolled open. I drove through and closed it behind me.

Jacque was seated at her desk in the outer office. Bob was seated on a corner of said desk. Both were smiling broadly.

"Here we go again," Jacque said. "You've been back at work what. Ten days? No, only nine, and already we're besieged by the press."

There was a knock at the front window and the front door. Three, maybe four reporters were outside, waving their arms to be let in.

"Don't worry," Jacque said. "I locked the door. You need coffee?"

"Oh yeah," I said. "By the bucketful. Let's load up and go into my office." And we did.

There was no real reason for me to be there, other than to see if Bob had found anything on Greenwood, which he hadn't; he was still working on it. But hell, it's my office and I enjoy it, so there I was, and there we were.

We chatted for maybe an hour, about this and that, the goings on at Harry Starke Investigations, and I silently thanked the lord that my two new partners had things well in hand.

Finally, when they could tell that my mind was elsewhere, they left me to my thoughts—and my third cup of coffee.

I tilted the big chair back as far as it would go, put my feet up on the desk, closed my eyes, and let the images run like a movie through my head. The next thing I knew that my phone was chirping and walking across the top of my desk.

I dropped my feet to the floor, let the chair tilt forward, and picked up the phone. It was the ME.

"Hey Doc," I said, and looked at my watch; it was almost noon. *Damn. I must have fallen asleep.* "How's it hangin'?" I asked, stealing his stock greeting.

"Hello to you too," he replied. "What's wrong with you, Harry? You sound… a bit strange."

"Nothing, I just have a lot on my mind. Did you watch the news last night and this morning?"

"I did. You're the man, Harry."

"'The man' my ass. I'm in my office besieged by reporters. Kate still with you?"

"No, she left some thirty minutes ago. I've just finished writing up my report on the Sandoval post. It's not good, Harry. Not good at all."

I nodded, even though I knew he couldn't see me. "So tell me."

"Well, it's much the same as the last one. The body had been washed. I found no trace evidence. Nothing. The undersides of her fingernails and toenails had been scraped clean. No hairs, no fibers, no semen. This person knows his forensics."

"How about the PMI?" I asked.

"Post mortem interval? Two days ago, two and a half at most. He must starve them. I wonder why. There was no gastric material in her stomach, so she hadn't eaten anything for at least three days. The skin is showing some marbling, lividity—in the buttocks, thighs, hands, ankles, and feet, but again, none in the back and shoulders." I heard him take a breath. "There are contusions and sticky residue on her ankles and arms, of the sort made by the application of duct tape. I think she spent her time in captivity, and after death, taped to a chair. Her eyes had been taped open and she had been strangled multiple times, like before. Time of death… sometime between noon and six in the evening on September eleventh."

"No signs of sexual assault?"

He hesitated. "There's superficial damage to the vagina and bruising on the inner thighs, but I found no semen. She was raped, at least once, but he must have used a condom."

I thought for a moment, wondering….

"Harry, are you still there?"

"Yeah, Doc. Sorry. Listen; you didn't by any chance find an injection site, did you?"

"No. Was I supposed to?"

"I don't know. Maybe."

"I'll take another look and let you know. If there's nothing else, I'll talk to you later."

"Okay. Later."

He disconnected.

I sat there for several minutes before I laid the phone down on my desk, and then picked it right back up again and called Kate.

"Hey," I said when she answered. "I'm under siege here. You want to come and pick me up?

Thirty minutes? Okay, good. You might want use a cruiser; there are sharks all around my offices."

It wasn't but a few minutes later when my phone buzzed again. I looked at the screen, then answered it.

"Hey, Doc. That was quick."

"You were right, Harry. How the hell I missed it I don't know. Must be getting old, I suppose. My eyesight's not what it was. I had to use a magnifying glass. Anyway, I found three injection sites. Two in the left buttock and one in the right."

"I sort of figured you might."

"Yes, well, so I thought I'd better take another look at the Hart girl… and I found two more." He paused, then continued, "We won't know what was injected until we get the toxicology report, but what are you thinking, Harry?"

"I'm not sure. I need to think about it. I'll let you know. Thanks, Doc."

Chapter 23

Twenty minutes later, my phone chirped. I looked at the screen—yeah, I was screening my calls—but it was only Kate, calling to tell me she was outside.

"Where to, Harry?" she asked as I slammed the car door behind me.

"Somewhere secluded…. Shit. We're being followed." And not just by one car. I counted three, and there may have been more.

"Yeah, I figured," she said, and then grinned at me, flipping on the blue lights and siren and hitting the gas. The big car lurched forward and we were soon in a reverse high-speed chase. The cruiser out front of four TV news cars, including one from Channel 7. I hoped to God Amanda wasn't in it.

Kate scorched down Georgia Avenue, hauled a tight right and ran a red light onto MLK, then a left onto Broad Street. From there the cruiser rocketed in and out of the traffic all the way to the I-24 interchange, then she was up the ramp and heading west toward Nashville at a speed that would have gotten me locked up for a month.

I watched out of the back window as our pursuers slowly dropped away. One gamely hung on for almost a mile, then he too gave it up, and we were free. Kate eased up on the gas, flipped off the lights and siren, and took a right off the interstate at Cummings Highway.

"The Cracker Barrel okay?" she asked. "I'm in the mood for some chicken and dumplings."

I thought about it, looked at my watch. It was 1:45.

"Yeah, why not. Shouldn't be too busy."

Wrong again. Those places are always busy. We stayed anyway. We grabbed a table at the far end of the restaurant where I could put my back to the wall and watch the door.

Kate ordered the chicken and dumplings, along with cornbread and unsweetened iced tea. Me? I ordered a bowl of pinto beans and cornbread and an iced tea, sweetened.

When we'd finished ordering and given back the menus, Kate sat back in her chair, folded her arms, and looked at me. No, she stared at me.

"What?" I asked.

"What the hell have you been up to? Never, *never*, in the almost seventeen years I've been a cop, have I had to run from the press like we just did."

I grinned at her. "I take it you didn't watch the news last night or this morning."

"I caught the tail end this mor-ning." She drew the word out as she figured it out. "Oh no. Not again? Emoji?"

I nodded. "Yes, 'fraid so, and it's going to make things difficult, to say the least."

The food arrived. She leaned forward and inhaled appreciatively over her plate. "Yummy."

At that, I had to laugh. Chicken and dumplings is not the least fattening food I could think of, and Kate had one hell of an appetite. How she managed to hang on to her shape I had no idea.... Yes I did. She worked out a hell of a lot.

"So," she said, her mouth full of dumplings. "What's so important we had run from the press?"

I looked down into my bowl of beans, stirred it with my spoon, then looked up at her and said, "I have something I want to run by you. It's been on my mind for a couple of days. It may or may not be anything, but I'd like to get your thoughts."

"Okay. Shoot."

"Kate, so far we've talked to just about everybody the three girls knew or were acquainted with. We have only one viable suspect, Joey Lister, but the case against him has more holes in it than a rusty bucket. So if we set him aside for a minute, where does that leave us? With nothing, right?"

"Where are you going with this, Harry?"

"Just bear with me a minute. We've talked to their friends, family.... Who else is there? What are we missing, do you think?"

She looked puzzled. She didn't answer.

I leaned forward over my bowl of beans.

"Apart from their family and friends," I said, "who would have known them better than anyone? Who would they have known and trusted enough to get into a car with them?"

"Go on," she said. "Tell me."

"Their professors."

"I already did! I talked to both of them, Doctor Douglas Wiggins and Doctor David Greenwood, when I got the Payne case. They both seemed harmless enough."

I nodded, and continued stirring my beans. "I told you I met someone the other night, at the club. Wanna guess who?"

"I… Jesus, Harry, I don't know. Who?"

"Dr. David Greenwood. Sneaky little bastard. He had the balls to come up to our table, and he insisted on being introduced to me… and Amanda. He struck me as one of those 'superior beings,' arrogant. You know the type. They talk down to everyone who doesn't have a PhD. I didn't like him, and I still can't for the life of me figure out what he wanted."

"Hero worship?" she asked, in a voice dripping with sarcasm. Then she shoved a big forkful of chicken and dumpling into her mouth.

"Maybe—" I grinned at her "—but I got the impression that it was more than that. I think he was on a fishing trip. He said he'd like to meet with me, to talk."

“So talk to him. You want me to come with you?”

I shook my head. “You said you talked to him,” I said. “Which is strange, because he never mentioned it. In fact, other than that he’d seen Amanda’s newscast, and that Emoji, and I quote, ‘intrigued him,’ he didn’t ask about the investigation at all.”

She nodded slowly. “So?”

“So what’s he up to? Why the interest?”

“I…. Oh hell, who knows? Okay, but I’m not buying it, that the professor did it in the library with the candlestick or whatever. For one thing, Greenwood wasn’t Maggie’s professor. Was he? Neither was Wiggins.”

I smiled at her. “No, he wasn’t, but he *was* her sister’s, Christie’s. They both were.”

She opened her mouth to speak, then closed it again and slowly shook her head. I had her.

I leaned forward and looked intently at her. “You said you talked to them. How? You interviewed them, right? But not as a suspects. You were looking for information. Who did the girls know? What were they like? Who were their friends, boyfriends, girlfriends, and so on? All of the usual background stuff. You didn’t question them as potential suspects.

“Kate, we have a link—a tenuous one, I agree, but a link nonetheless. They were all psychology majors… well, three of them were, and I know for a fact that Maggie Hart knew both of them. Not well, but well enough to share a coffee and a chat on several occasions. Maybe…. What?"

She was shaking her head. "I still don't see it. There's no friggin' way. I thought Greenwood was nice… well, he was to *me*."

Oh yeah? I wonder why? I thought sarcastically.

"I thought he was a dear," she continued, "a sweetheart. A bit weird, maybe, but he doesn't have it in him…."

"Jeez, Kate. You didn't meet the same Greenwood I met then. But go on."

"Well, then… and Wiggins… he's also weird, but not really that kind of weird either. I think you're wrong, Harry."

"Kate, as long as we worked together, as long as you were my partner, what two things did I try to impress upon you the most?"

She didn't even hesitate. "Keep an open mind, and killers come in all sorts of shapes and sizes… I get it, Harry, but these two? You'll have to see for yourself; you'll have to talk to them."

"I already talked to Greenwood. Remember?" I said dryly. "But okay. We'll talk to them. In fact, I'll take Greenwood up on his invitation. You can accompany me." I looked at my watch. It was already after three. "But not today. How about I try to set something up for first thing tomorrow morning?"

She nodded.

"You have his number?"

She did. I tapped it into my phone.

"Dr. Greenwood," I said lightly. "Your invitation to talk, I'd like to take you up on it, if I may. Can we get together tomorrow morning, say ten o'clock?"

"Um, er, ten, you say? I'll be in my clinic most of the morning. Let me take a look at my schedule."

I heard the phone being put down. A minute later he was back on.

"No, that won't work," he said. "I have patients all morning, and I have classes to teach in the afternoon and evening. I do have a thirty-minute break at noon. Will that do?"

I told him it would, thanked him, and disconnected.

"So," I said. "Tomorrow at noon. What are you doing the rest of the day?"

"Me? Back to work, I suppose. You?"

I thought about it for a minute, then said, "Me too. I need to go to the office. My car's there, for one thing, and I need to talk to Jacque and Bob. D'you mind dropping me off?"

"If I don't, you'll have to walk," she said, smiling.

"Better that than the shark tank in front of my office."

But the tank was empty. The vans and cars had all gone, all but one, and that one I recognized right away. A red Jaguar F-Type SUV. Amanda's.

I found her in the back office talking to Jacque and Bob.

I gave her a peck on the cheek. She pulled away, obviously bothered about something.

"What?" I asked. "Who kicked your cat?"

"What the hell was Kate thinking?" she asked. "She might have killed someone, or you, or both. I was in the Channel 7 car. I had to tell Jerry to pull over. I'm almost certain that stunt she pulled was illegal. What? What the hell are you laughing about?"

"I was laughing at the thought of you out there circling with the rest of the sharks."

"It's not funny. We have a job to do. Sometimes things can get a little… intense, but… it's what we do. You know that."

"Ah, I see," I said, nodding sagely. "Obviously, my dear, you have never been on the receiving end of one of the feeding frenzies you and your compatriots engage in. You're like a tank full of piranhas. Hell, Amanda, Jacque had to lock all the doors. Anyway, I wasn't having any of it. See? I don't have to talk to the press; not ever, and… I won't! Not ever!"

At that she seemed to calm down a little. She sighed, nodded, tilted her head and looked sideways at me. *Uh, oh! Here it comes.*

"Harry…."

"Don't even go there," I said, noting that both Jacque and Bob were smiling.

"Time we left these two alone, I tink," Jacque said, sliding playfully into her Jamaican twang. "Come, Bob. I tink there's maybe some makeup sex about to be happ'nin."

"Get outta here." I picked up a file from the desk and swung at her lightly, but missed. She darted out the door, still laughing. "Hey, Bob, wait," I said. "What did you find?"

"I'm still putting it together. Tomorrow morning okay?"

It was, and he left too.

"I told you," I said to Amanda, as the door closed behind them, "Don't go there…." But she did. She turned the lock and….

***

That night they came to me again, the four of them. They didn't say anything. They never did. They just stood silently beside the bed, looking down at me reproachfully.

I don't know whether I was awake or not, but when I woke again to the sound of the alarm I had the distinct memory that I had asked them what they wanted. If they'd answered, I had no memory of it. They seemed real enough, but I knew they were just a dream. What was it Scrooge had called Marley's ghost? An undigested bit of beef, a blob of mustard, a crumb of cheese, a fragment of underdone potato? Yeah, that was it, I think.

Whatever. If the girls replied or not, I don't remember it. I did, however, get the feeling that they wanted something. To rest in peace, perhaps, which would only be possible once I…. Well, I'd do my best.

I didn't run that morning. Instead I settled for fifty laps in the pool. Then I ate a light breakfast of scrambled eggs and coffee and left for the office. I wanted to check in with Bob, see what he'd found out about the Greenwoods.

Chapter 24

It seemed like it had been years since I'd spent any time in my private office—my cave, as Kate used to call it. It was my refuge, a place where I could relax and spend an undisturbed hour or two, a place to think. If the door was closed my people usually knew not to disturb me, but not that day. At around nine o'clock, someone knocked.

I can't say it bothered me, but I sighed when I got up to open it.

"Sorry boss," Bob said, "but I thought you'd like to see what I found out yesterday."

I nodded. "Sure. Come on in. Take a load off."

He dropped a thin file on my desk and sat down. There wasn't much to the file, just a few sheets of paper, a credit report, and a computer disk.

I flipped through the pages. It was mostly background stuff.

Dr. David and Mrs. Shari Greenwood met in 1998 while they were both studying Experimental Psychology at University College, Oxford. Apparently David saw something quite special in the pretty American girl because, following a whirlwind romance of only three weeks, they were married in a registry office in Brighton. *Either that or he was after her money... or maybe a green card.*

At the time, David was twenty-three and Shari a year younger.

The Greenwoods were indeed quite well off, the bulk of the wealth belonging to Shari, the only child of Michael and Toni Marshall. Her mother died from breast cancer in 2001, and she inherited everything when her father died in a small aircraft accident in 2003. The family company, SETO, the acronym for Southeast Tennessee Oil Company, owned, among other things, some twenty-eight SETO One Stop convenience stores in and around the city and Hamilton County. The company also owned a bulk oil depot located on Jersey Pike from which they supplied only their own stores with gas. Shari Greenwood was a very wealthy woman.

Early in his career at UTC David Greenwood had published, as all academics are required to do, a treatise—several of them in fact, but one in particular caught my eye. It seems the good doctor had spent an inordinate amount of time studying fear.

His theory was regarded as controversial, and it wasn't well received by his peers, but that wasn't what grabbed my attention. It was the subject: fear. *Now there's a thing. We should talk to him about that. What did Doc say? Her eyes had been taped open? That means the killer must have been looking into them when he killed her.... Fear? Oh yeah. We need to talk to him about that.*

Both Greenwoods had clean records, not even a parking ticket between them, although there had been an allegation of professional misconduct against Dr. G. in 2006. It involved a female patient at his clinic and hypnosis. Nothing ever came of it; money changed hands and the allegation was quietly dropped.

So, the good doctor has a little problem, methinks. Can't keep his hands to himself.

Greenwood and his wife lived in a luxury three-story home on Riverview overlooking the golf course, not too far from where my father lives.

"Okay," I said. "There are some questions here that need to be answered." I dropped the file down the desk.

"There are?" Bob asked. "And what might they be?"

"About Greenwood and the fear thing, for one. What was that about?"

"I don't really know. He published a paper on it years ago. I downloaded it, but I didn't read it. It was way beyond me, but…. Well, you have that fancy degree, so maybe you can make something of it. I included it in the file."

"You did? I didn't see it."

"It's on that disk in the sleeve. Fifty pages of technical crap I couldn't make heads or tails of."

"Okay. I'll read it through later. What about this settlement for misconduct?"

"A something and nothing thing, as far as I could discover. Mrs. G. paid the woman a substantial sum—the amount was undisclosed—and charges were never brought against him. The girl concerned seems to have disappeared. No, no," he said, as I opened my mouth to speak. "That was part of the deal. She had to move away and keep her mouth shut. I'll have Tim try and track her down if you want."

I thought about it. "Yeah. Do that. Maybe we can get her to talk. Anything else?"

"Hmmm. Maybe, but…." He paused, a huge grin on his face.

"What? Don't screw around. Tell me. Give it to me."

He reached into the inside pocket of his jacket, drew out a folded sheet of paper, and handed it to me.

"What is it?" I asked as I opened it. "Oh! Hey! Wow!"

"Yeah, I thought you'd like that. That's why I kept it for last."

"Friggin' hell, Bob." I looked across the desk at him. He was grinning like a barracuda: all teeth, eyes glistening.

"A 1976 Chevy Silverado…. You've got to be friggin' kidding me."

He shook his head, still grinning. "You ain't done yet. Keep reading."

"Oh no way! No friggin' way. A 2016 Nissan Rogue. His wife has a friggin' silver Rogue?"

He cackled. "Yeah, *boy*! She has a Mercedes sports car too and he has a Mercedes E300, but…."

I sat there staring at the piece of paper. I was stunned. It wasn't possible. Things like that just don't happen.

I looked up at him. He cocked his head sideways and raised his eyebrows. "So?" he asked.

"So. It's him. It's gotta be. We need that truck, and the Rogue. If we can tie either or both of them to the victims…. I need to call Kate."

She picked up on the second ring. "What?" she snapped. "I'm heading to your office literally right now. I am putting on my coat."

"Kate." I just couldn't keep it to myself. "You're not going to believe this: I know who the killer is. It's Greenwood."

"*Shut… up*!" She all but exploded. "How the hell…?"

"I'll tell you when I get there," I interrupted her. "Don't leave. I'll be there as soon as I can."

It was almost 10:15 when I did finally make it to her office, and she wasn't alone. Chief Johnston was sitting in front of her desk.

"I hear you have good news, Harry," he boomed. "Lieutenant Gazzara tells me you think you have

Emoji, that he's a UTC professor. I find that hard to believe, but I'm ready to listen. Do tell."

It wasn't exactly what I needed right then, but I had no choice, so I laid it out. It took more than an hour. When I had finished, I looked from Kate to the chief and back. Kate was in a state of total disbelief; like me, she couldn't get over the coincidence that the Greenwoods owned vehicles matching those we were looking for.

Chief Johnston? He didn't say a whole lot. He sat the whole time with his elbows on the arms of his chair and his fingers steepled.

"It sounds… reasonable," he said, after a moment of silence. "But a doctor. A professor. I hope you've got it right. If you don't, the repercussions could be… well, we won't go there, at least not now."

He rose to his feet. So did I. So did Kate.

"Be good, people," he said, "be very good. Don't screw it up."

Kate and I spent the next two hours going over everything we had, which when it came right down to it was very little. We had two likely vehicles and my dislike of David Greenwood, and that was about it.

By two thirty that afternoon, we'd dragged Lonnie into the mix, read Greenwood's paper—well, Kate and I had—and we'd talked it to death. There was nothing more we could do until we'd talked to him and, while we could have busted in on him, we decided to wait until the appointment we had scheduled with him for the next day.

That decided, I left Kate and Lonnie to it, and went home to swim, drink, eat steak, and make love to my wife. And I did all of them, twice, some three times—drink and swim, that is. I ate only one steak, and I managed.... Oh hell. You don't need to know that.

Chapter 25

I arrived at the Police Services Center on Amnicola just before nine that Friday morning. Kate was in her office, talking to Lonnie; even from the hallway she looked exhausted. When she saw me she waved for me to join them. I did.

For about thirty minutes we talked it through—again—and again we came to the conclusion that there was little more we could do until we'd talked to Greenwood.

At 11:45, Kate and I left the PD and headed for Vine Street. We arrived at Greenwood's clinic a few minutes before noon.

"So. How do you want to handle this?" she asked as we walked up the front steps.

"Just stay quiet and follow my lead. If I need your help, I'll give you a nod."

He was waiting for us at the front door.

"Come in, come in," he enthused as he opened the door. "It's so good of you to take the time, Mr. Starke.... Oh. You're not alone, I see. And who is this young lady?"

"This is Lieutenant Catherine Gazzara. She's with the major crimes unit, Homicide Division, Chattanooga Police Department," I said, hoping that providing him with the full introduction would either impress or intimidate him. It did neither.

"Ah," he said, extending his hand. "It's so nice to meet you, Lieutenant—" he pronounced it "Leftenant"—"but why, I have to wonder, are you here?"

"This is not a social visit, Doctor. We're investigating a series of murders—all students at UTC. And all but one are psychology students, your students."

"Ah-ha," he said, nodding and smiling. "I see. Well let's get to it then, shall we? Follow me, please."

We followed him through to what I supposed must be his consulting room. There was a couch, a coffee table, four rather formal antique armchairs, several pieces of original artwork on the walls, and not much else.

"Please. Do sit down. Would you like some tea, coffee, or something cool, perhaps?"

"Nothing thank you, Doctor." I said. Kate shook her head too.

He nodded, sat down in one of the chairs, crossed his legs, set his elbows on the arms of his chair, steepled his fingers, lowered his chin, and tilted his head slightly to one side. "So. What can I do for you?"

"How well did you know Margaret Hart, Doctor?"

"Ah. She is one of the victims I've been reading about. Is that correct?"

"It is," I replied.

"But she was not one of my students. How would I know her?"

"Her sister, Christie, *is* one of your students, and she says you knew her quite well."

He was shaking his head. "I… don't… *think*…. Oh, yes, of course, you're talking about Maggie." He paused, then seemed shocked. "She was…. No! I don't believe it. It was her? She's dead?" I watched his eyes. They never so much as flickered, but there was something there: the eyelids were slightly closed and he was staring at me intently. "Yes. I did know her, but only in passing. I joined the two of them for coffee, twice, I believe."

"How about Chloe Sandoval? She *was* one of your students. We found her body yesterday morning."

His eyes narrowed even further. "Where are you going with this, Mr. Starke? Am I to suppose that I'm a suspect of some kind?"

I ignored the question and pressed on. I flipped the lock screen on my iPad, looked up at him, and said, "You own a 1976 Chevrolet Silverado pickup truck, right?"

"I did, yes."

I looked sharply at him. "You did? Where is it now?"

"I don't know. It was stolen from one of our franchises some seven or eight months ago." *Oh hell. Sure it was.*

"Did you report it stolen, Doctor?"

"I'm afraid I didn't."

"Why not?"

He shrugged. "Well, it was quite old, going rusty, you know. It only worth a few hundred dollars, perhaps, and hardly worth the inconvenience. We kept it at one of our lube shops, just used it to haul odd bits and pieces around. My wife, Shari, was glad to see it gone; she regarded it as an eyesore. Can't say I blame her really." Then he looked me right in the eye and said, "And… it was a sickening shade of baby-shit green."

Holy Mary mother of God. It's you!

I didn't want him to catch my reaction, though I'm sure he did, so I flipped through a couple of screens, then asked him, "Where were you on the evening of Wednesday August thirtieth between five thirty and six thirty?"

"Good God, man. How the hell should I know? That was three weeks ago. Home, I should think. Eating dinner. You'll have to ask my wife."

"And…" I flipped some more, "how about on September eighth? Where were you between nine thirty and ten thirty that evening?"

He didn't even bother to think. He gave a sly smile and said, quietly, with no little hint of innuendo. “That one’s easy, Mr. Starke. I was at the club, having drinks with your father.”

Now that did knock me back, and he knew it. *Oh... my... God.*

“Come on, Doctor,” I said, trying to gather my thoughts. “You can’t remember where you were three weeks ago, but you don’t even have to think about where you were two weeks ago? I’m not buying it.”

“You don’t have to. I’m sure August will confirm it. But he really doesn’t have to. You see, I have it in writing. We played a little poker that night. August lost. He wrote a check. I deposited it the following morning and… oh yes, he did date it.”

Son of a bitch. He’s playing with me. Teasing, testing me. Time to move on, take back the initiative.

“Doctor,” I said, as lightly as I could manage, “some years ago you published a somewhat serious work on fear. I read it. Several times in fact. I found it to be a little… shall we say… out there. Your premise was that fear is the result of a hormone imbalance and could easily be eradicated by an injection of a substance you declined to name. In fact, I seem to recall it was ridiculed by your colleagues. That must have hurt.”

“Hmmm,” he said. “I assume you’re leaning on that master’s degree you have from Fairleigh Dickenson, a somewhat *lightweight* university, so I’m told.”

Lightweight? You friggin' dirtbag. Lightweight my ass.

"Oh don't look so surprised," he continued. "Just like you, Mr. Starke, I do my research. I'm very much afraid, though, that your master's degree—criminal psychology, isn't it?—is woefully lacking in depth. What a waste of five years. Or was it six?"

I ignored the son of a bitch.

"Ah, cat got your tongue? Well, in any case, your knowledge of the subject is at best narrow-minded and at worst, woefully ill-informed. For many years, those who should know better have maintained the idea that fear is generated by the amygdala, but they're wrong, Mr. Starke. Wrong. Fear is in fact the product of specific cognitive structures in the neocortex that function *in parallel* with the amygdala. It's a subtle distinction between the conscious and unconscious aspects of fear, to be sure, but an important one, don't you think?"

"And the injection? What about that?"

He shrugged. "As you said, the idea was ridiculed, so I moved on." He paused, stared at me for a moment, then said thoughtfully, "Hmmm, I wonder."

"You wonder about what? And please, tell me about the injection."

"I told you. I moved on. There is no injection. There is, however, something I'd like to ask you. There is something quite fascinating about death, don't you think? Oh I know you do, Mr. Starke. For instance: is it the end of an existence and the beginning of a new one—or just some sort of moving on? I'm particularly interested to know what happens to the 'you' when you die. The true you, you understand. The consciousness. The *soul*. Are you not also fascinated, Mr. Starke? I understand that quite recently you yourself almost died…."

"We're here to ask questions, Doctor, not to answer them. Now, if you don't cooperate, I'll have Lieutenant Gazzara transport you to the police department and we can continue the interview there, which would be a total waste of your time and mine, so why don't you help me out here?"

He stared at me in silence for a moment, then glanced at Kate, and then back at me.

"I have followed your career with some interest, Mr. Starke. You're a fascinating character, and something of an enigma. You're extremely wealthy, and thus have no need to immerse yourself in death in all its forms, but you do. You also appear to be quite a clever individual, but you make mistakes, mistakes that sometimes hurt the ones you love. I'll tell you what I'm prepared to do. I'll answer your questions if you will answer mine. Deal?"

"No, Doctor. No deal. Like I told you, I'm investigating a string of murders, and I have the feeling I've found my killer. That would be you, Professor Greenwood. Now, will you please answer my questions?"

He laughed aloud. “Me? *Me?* Oh my, oh my. How absolutely delicious….” He stared at me, his mouth open, his eyes smiling, “You’re serious. *Me*? A serial murder? Yes, yes, yes, I like it.” He held out his hands to be cuffed. “Take me to the—what is it you call it?—the slammer.”

I, of course, had no cuffs, and Kate didn’t oblige him.

“It’s you, isn’t it Doctor,” I said quietly. “You’re Emoji. It’s the fear thing, right?”

He slowly lowered his hands, then he laughed, but the humor was gone. “What on earth are you talking about, Mr. Starke? Me? Emoji? That’s just too funny.”

“I notice you’re not denying it,” I said.

“What’s to deny? I’ve never heard anything so ridiculous in my life.” His face hardened; his eyes turned into narrow slits of ice blue. “And that’s one hell of an accusation you’re making, Mr. Starke. Let’s see if you’re smart enough to prove it. Either arrest me, or get the hell out of my clinic and don’t come back, you tiresome wanker. Much worthier men than you have tried to best me. They all failed, and so will you.”

And then he smiled again. His eyes widened and the ice retreated into the palest shade of blue. He tilted his head sideways, and then the smile hardened and the eyes narrowed again. The look on his face was one of pure evil and, at that precise moment, I was certain that I had found my killer, and that he wasn't going to stop killing until I nailed him.

I nodded, rose slowly to my feet, and said, equally quietly, "No one is that good, Doctor. Maybe instead of fear you should study the ego and *its* effects on the brain. It's a powerful stimulant; I suggest you try not to overdose. It could be your undoing." And we left him, still smiling, his wrists still pressed together between his knees.

***

"Well?" Kate asked when we got outside.

"It's him."

"Even though he was with your father the night Chloe was abducted?"

"I don't care. It's him. He pulled it off somehow."

"How do you know?"

"I feel it."

"Oh hell." She shook her head. "Here we go again. You *feel* it?"

"Yeah, I feel it."

"It may not be him, Harry. The truck, the car, and your *gut feeling*. That's all we have, and right now the truck and car are circumstantial at best. The feeling?" She shook her head. "I have another theory that fits much better."

"You *do?* No way. Tell me."

"Okay. How about this. I'm thinking we have a better shot with Haskins and Lister working together. The truck is the right color, we can put at least one victim inside it, and Lister has a late-model Rogue."

"Nah," I said. "It's him. It's Greenwood."

"Harry, he has an *alibi*!" She shook her head and pressed the heels of her hands into her eyes. For a long moment, she was silent. I couldn't see her face to read her. Then she sucked in a deep breath, groaned, and dropped her hands. "Okay. Have it your way. What now?"

"We go see his frigging wife is what. Right now. And I want to search the damned house. We need to find that truck, and we need to impound the Rogue. We need a warrant."

I called Judge Strange.

"Henry," I said, without preamble, "I'm working the Emoji case with Kate Gazzara. We need a warrant to search Dr. David Greenwood's home and impound his wife's car, and I need it now. Can you do it, please?"

I've known Henry for more years than I can remember. He's a member of the club and one of my weekend golfing buddies. My relationship with the judge was such that we both knew we could rely on each other to provide what we needed in a pinch and, over the years, I had done most of the providing. I knew he'd come through for me… only he didn't.

"Greenwood, you say? Hmmm. I know him. He's a member of the club. I've played poker with him, several times. Always a winner, that one. I often wonder if he's a cheat. Why do you want to search his home, Harry?"

I spent the next five minutes explaining why, and he spent one minute explaining why not.

"Sounds to me like you want to go fishing, Harry. All you have is a missing truck, his wife's car, and a feeling. It's not enough. I can't do it, Harry. The man has an alibi for at least one of the murders, for Christ's sake; you don't have probable cause. Come back to me when you have something more. You on for golf this weekend?"

I was stunned. That was a first. But when I thought about it, I realized he was right. A bum warrant is not worth two cents. "I dunno," I said. "I'll let you know. See you, Henry."

"No go, huh?" Kate asked. "Now what?"

"I honestly don't know."

"What about Wiggins? You want to interview him?"

"Nah. There's no point. It's not him, or any of the others either. It's Greenwood. I know it, and he knows I know it. And he's taunting us… well, me. We need to find that truck."

"How about the wife? You still want to talk to her?"

"Yeah, I do, but not right now. There's no point. He's established his alibi. She can't corroborate it; only August can do that, and I know he will. Let's go buy him lunch." I looked at my watch. It was a few minutes after one o'clock. "I'd better call him first, though. You never know where he is or what he's up to."

I called his cell phone; it went straight to voicemail, so I called, Alice, his secretary.

"He's in court all day," she told me. "Can I have him call you when he gets a free moment?"

I told her she could, and disconnected. *So much for that.*

But he did call me back, though it was late the following morning, by which time the world had turned upside down.

Chapter 26

Saturday the sixteenth was a black day for me, and for Lindsey Scott.

I don't usually work weekends, but what with Emoji and all, I figured I needed to try to find a way to get to Greenwood, so I headed into the office. I was going through what we had, which wasn't a whole lot, when Jacque walked in and handed me a large brown envelope.

"This came for you a few minutes ago," she said, then turned to leave.

"Whoa woah woah, wait a minute. Came how? You already got the mail from post office, so…"

"Someone must have dropped it off. I went to the bathroom and when I came back, it was on my desk."

"Well surely Leslie or Margo must have seen who it was," I said, peeling back the sticky flap. My heart was already beating too fast; I knew what was in the envelope. I would have bet money on it.

"Sorry. Leslie's not working today, and Margo's at Staples buying pens."

"Damn!" I pulled the single sheet of paper from its confines and stared down it; sure enough, the emoji smiled up at me. *Bring it on.* The number three was written in thick black marker between its beckoning fingers.

I slammed the piece of paper down on the desk and stared at it. It stared back at me, the mocking smile turning my guts to water. *The bastard has another one*.

I reached for my phone, but before I could pick it up, it rang. I looked at the screen. It was Kate.

"He has another one," I said, even before she could speak.

"You'd better get over here," she said. She sounded terrible, like she was halfway to death herself. "The chief's on his way to my office and he's bringing the two FBI guys with him. I think the shit's about to hit the fan."

"I'll be there as soon as I can. There's something I have to do here first—Kate? *Kate*?" She wasn't there. She'd hung up.

"Jacque," I said—she was still standing by the open door—"I need to check the cameras. Where's Tim?"

"His office, far as I know."

I pushed myself to my feet and headed over.

"Hey Boss—" Tim started, but I didn't even let him get the rest of it out.

"Run the cameras back for me," I told him. "Just the last thirty minutes."

He did. Slowly.

"Sheesh, Tim. I don't have all day. Speed them up." I watched as the six images on the single forty-four-inch screen flickered by.

"Whoa. Stop. That one," I pointed. "Back it up… go… go… stop! Now run it at normal speed."

It was the security camera on the corner of the front of the building. There he was, a man, walking away from the camera toward the front door of the outer office. He was wearing jeans, one of those brightly colored Hawaiian shirts, and a straw cowboy hat with a wide brim. Unfortunately, his back was to the camera and the brim of the hat was pulled low over his eyes. Without looking around, he ducked in through the front door.

"The interior camera, Tim. Pull it up."

He did, but the image wasn't much better. The man was in the office no more than four seconds. He was hunched low, the crown of the hat facing the camera. He dropped the envelope on the desk, spun on his heel, and was gone. If we hadn't been looking for him, we'd have missed him.

"Go back to the outside camera. Maybe he…." But he didn't. He reappeared through the front door with his head down, shoulders hunched, hands in the pockets of his jeans, back to the camera, and disappeared down Georgia toward MLK.

Damn! Damn! Damn! I stared at the image of his retreating back. *It's the right height, the right build…. It's him. It has to be.*

"Thanks, Tim. Put it all on a thumb drive for me, please. It's not going to help any. At least I don't think it is, but…."

"You want me to dig a little? You never know."

"Yeah. Why not. Can't hurt. Shit. Alright, I gotta go."

***

I walked into the situation room at the police department to find it in turmoil. People were talking and shouting across desks; computer screens were filled with the image of the evil emoji. Across the room, through the window to Kate's office, I could see her standing behind her desk, waving her arms and talking animatedly to someone I couldn't see.

I knocked on the door. It was opened by no less than Chief Johnston himself.

"There you are," he growled. "Come in. Where the hell have you been?"

Special Agent Caster was standing with his back to the wall, facing Kate's desk. Agent Mendez was absent.

"In my office, Chief. In my office. D'you have a problem with that?" If he did, I didn't care. It was because of him that I'd turned in my ticket almost ten years ago. He could bully me no longer. How the hell Kate could continue to put up with it…. Ah hell. It's easy for me. For her, not so much.

"It's over, Starke. Agent Caster is taking over from—"

"Fine," I interrupted him. "See you, Kate. Call me if you need me."

I turned and walked out of the office, the back of my head hiding a smile I didn't really feel, but screw 'em.

"Starke!" The great voice boomed out over the incident room. "What the hell d'you think you're doing? Get your ass back in here *now*!"

I stopped. I grinned at the startled faces of the clerks, detectives, and uniforms, then turned, walked back into Kate's office, and closed the door behind me."

"What?" I asked. "You just handed the case over to the Green Lantern here—" I nodded in Caster's direction, also noting the sly smile on Kate's face "—so you don't need me anymore. No, I can go back to work. I have things I need to catch up on. Call me if you need me." And I turned again to the door.

"Sit your ass down, Harry," the chief said quietly.

"Caster's taking over. I have no choice."

"I want the files, Starke," Caster said. "All of them."

"Screw you, Caster. What few files I have are here." I tapped my forehead. "And you're not getting them."

"I don't believe you. I want them and I want them in the next sixty minutes. If I don't get them, I'll slap you with a subpoena and a search warrant."

“So slap me with one,” I said. “Henry Strange will issue an injunction five minutes later. You’re not winning this one, *Gordy*, so back the hell off. I don’t work for you and I don’t work for Johnston. Work the case if you want, but as far as I’m concerned, you’re on your own.”

He stared at me, his lips a thin tight line, then he shook his head, stalked out of the office door, and slammed it behind him.

“Now,” I said, sitting down in front of Kate’s desk. “Where were we?”

“Jesus, Harry,” Johnston said, dropping into the seat beside me. “I hope to hell you know what you’re doing. That’s one mean son of a bitch you just blew off.”

I grinned at him. “You’re not exactly Willie Wonka yourself, Chief.”

At that he grinned. “It’s Greenwood, right?” he asked. “Don’t worry. I haven’t told Caster. How sure are you, Harry? Can you get him before Caster does?”

“If Caster doesn’t know. Maybe. But to answer your question: yes, I’m sure. Very sure. But can I prove it? No. Not even a little bit.”

I took the folded paper from my pocket. “Look, I got this about an hour ago. The son of a bitch had the balls to drop it off at my office personally.”

I held it out to Johnston, and he snatched it from me. "Why the hell didn't you grab him, for Christ's sake?"

"We didn't see him. He was in and out in just a couple of seconds. The only reason I know it was him is because of the security cameras; they don't show his face, but it *was* him."

He shook his head, frustrated.

"We have another one, right?" I asked Kate.

She nodded, picked up several sheets of paper from her desk, and said, "Lindsey Scott. She's nineteen, a freshman and a psych major. She was reported missing at—well, we got the word here at just after nine thirty this morning. The emojis arrived a few minutes after. If the pattern holds true, we have three days."

"The son of a bitch is playing with us," I said.

"I need this finished, Harry," Johnston said. "I had the mayor on the phone earlier, and he wants the TBI to handle it. I told him no, but he went over my head. Close it out, Harry, and soon." He shook his head again, then got up and left the office.

"You've got balls, Harry," Kate said. "I'll give you that. Whatever pull you had with the TBI, you just flushed it down the pot. It was fun to watch, though. I wish I had that kind of clout."

I shrugged. "Never mind about Caster. My pull is in Nashville, with Condon, not the Knoxville regional office. Now, what about Lindsey Scott?"

Unfortunately, there was nothing. Nothing new, anyway. She was missing, and that was all we had, except that I knew that David Greenwood had her hidden away somewhere. But where…?

My father called on his way out of court. It was a quick call, the way they usually are when the old man is working a case. He did, however, confirm that Greenwood was with him, Larry Spruce, and Robert Sinclair, from eight in the evening until almost eleven. They were playing Texas hold 'em, just like Greenwood had said.

"We know he has her," I said once I'd hung up, "the question is where. We have less than three days to figure it out, Kate. We have to find her. I can't handle another dead kid."

"So what are you thinking?"

"Well first we need to get out of here, away from Elliot Ness and his buddy. Let's go to my place."

She looked at me sharply.

"My office, Kate. My office."

She nodded. "Go ahead. I'll follow you. I'll be there in twenty or thirty minutes."

I nodded and headed out the door… and immediately turned around and walked back in again. "I changed my mind. I'm going to see Greenwood. You up for it?"

She looked at me for a moment, then smiled. It was a slow, wide thing, all teeth. "Hell yeah. Your car or mine?"

"Both. We can drop yours off at my office. I need to have a quick word with Tim first, and then we'll go and do a little bear baiting."

It took less than five minutes to tell Tim what I needed. I could have done it by phone, but I needed to make sure he had it right. I needed him to run a thorough search of the SETO finances, bank accounts, offshore accounts, properties, whatever.

That done, I went back to the outer office. Kate had arrived and was talking with Bob. The conversation stopped abruptly when I walked in.

I grinned. "You two on again or off again?"

"Off," Kate said, at the same time Bob said, "On."

"I see," I said. "You really should get your acts together. You'd make a lovely couple. Let's go, Lieutenant."

Kate was looking angry when she sank into the Beast's leather passenger seat.

"Did I hit a nerve?" I asked with a smile.

"I'll hit a nerve if you don't shut up and drive."

So I did.

***

You know how you can work yourself into a state of euphoria, thinking about and rehearsing what you're going to say to someone? Well that was me on the way to Vine Street. I mulled over the words, twisted them around and around, until finally I'd worked myself up into a good old state of *look the hell out, here I come.*

I ran up the front steps of the building—Kate following close behind—burst in through the front door, bypassed the reception desk and its occupant, and slammed open the door to his inner sanctum. He was seated behind his desk doing something on his computer, and reared back in his chair when we came in.

"What the…."

"Harry," Kate said, grabbing my arm, "don't."

I shrugged her off. I darted forward, leaned over the desk, grabbed Greenwood by his shirt, and dragged him up and over the top of the desk. I put my face so close to his I could smell the peppermint on his breath.

"Where is she, you sick piece of garbage?" And that was not at all what I'd rehearsed.

"What? What are you talking about?" he asked quietly—too quietly. He looked me right in the eyes. I could see he was shaken, but not all that much, and he sure wasn't frightened of me, not even a little bit.

Maybe there's something to his theory, I thought.

But I knew right away that he knew exactly what I was talking about.

I let him go. He sank back down into his seat, steepled his fingers against his lips, and looked up at me. He tilted his head to one side, lowered his chin, and smiled at me.

"Well, are you going to tell me what this is all about, or are you not?" he asked.

"Where is she, David? Where is Lindsey Scott?"

"Oh dear oh dear," he said, without taking his eyes off mine. "Are you telling me that another of my students has disappeared?"

I stared at him. "I didn't say that. How did you know she was one of your students?"

His eyebrows rose, and the smile widened; he began nodding slowly. "Nice one. If I'd been your man, you would have had me for that little slip of the tongue.... But it wasn't a slip, was it?" he asked. "It was, after what we discussed during our last interview, no more than an innocent enquiry. You'll have to do better than that, Mr. Starke."

I had to admit it. He was right: I would have to do better. For now, though, all I could do was try the direct approach. An appeal.

I looked him in the eye. "Please don't do this again," I pleaded. "She's only nineteen. She's just a baby. Where is she? Where's Lindsey?" It was a forlorn hope, and really quite a stupid thing to do, considering I knew the man to be a stone-cold killer, but what the hell.

Maybe, I thought, *he'll let something slip.*

He didn't. His eyes never left mine. He stared at me, unblinking, unsmiling, then said, "I haven't the foggiest idea."

I sighed, and nodded, and turned away from him.

"C'mon, Lieutenant," I said. "Let's go. It stinks in here."

Chapter 28

I left Greenwood's clinic in one of the blackest moods I can remember ever being in. I needed a drink, and I wasn't looking for water. I knew of only one place where I could find what I was looking for at four in the afternoon, and it was a dark hole in the wall with a bar and cheap liquor. Yeah, the Sorbonne.

The place was empty. It was, after all, only just after four o'clock. Benny Hinkle was on his own behind the bar, a glass in one hand and a filthy cloth in the other.

"Ah hell!" He threw down the cloth and returned the glass to the murky water in the sink. "What the hell have I done to deserve this? Hi Kate. You want a drink?" Then to me: "You can get the hell outta here. You never bring nothin' but trouble."

"Shut the hell up, Benny, and pour me a scotch. In a foam cup. A *new* one!"

He looked wounded, but he did what I asked, then flipped the top off a Corona and handed it to Kate.

"What do you want Harry?" he asked.

"Strangely enough, Benny, not a damned thing. Just a drink and few minutes of peace and quiet."

"It's that Emoji thing, right? I heard you two had been stiffed with that one. Any progress?"

I stared at him. He was Chattanooga's answer to Danny DeVito only fatter, dirty, and balder. I was about to hand him a smart answer, but then I caught the sympathy in his eyes. We go back a long way, Benny and me, good times and bad. Well, mostly bad, but the sparring we always engaged in had no edge to it.

"No, Benny," I sighed. "No progress. Not yet."

"You need to catch him, Harry. Young girls… sheesh." He shook his head and walked away.

Me? I nodded, looked at Kate, then turned and went to one of the darkened booths and sat down. She followed and sat down opposite.

"You shouldn't let him get to you, Harry," she said quietly, and sipped her beer.

"Who, Benny? He didn't. He's actually pretty okay."

"No. Not Benny. Greenwood."

I nodded. "Oh. Yep, he got to me, the cold-blooded son of a bitch.

I drank only a couple sips of the scotch. It was enough. I pushed the glass away and stood up.

"Let's go and see if Tim found anything."

***

What Tim had found wasn't a whole lot more than what we already had. The company was clean, paid its taxes, and had no offshore accounts or dealings. But what Tim also had was a list of the SETO properties, and they were extensive.

Apart from the thirty-odd SETO One Stop convenience stores and lube shops, the company was heavily into rental properties: apartments, houses, strip malls.

"Jeez," I said, handing Kate the list. "There are more than two hundred listings here. Where the hell do we start?" And as soon as I said it, I had an epiphany. "Lube shops! They have lube shops. Greenwood said the truck was stolen from a lube shop. How many do they have?"

She consulted the list. "Three."

"Three? That's all? Let's go check 'em out."

"Right now, tonight? I can't. It's already twenty after six, and there's something I have to do that I can't get out of."

I stared at her. "Kate, the clock is ticking."

"I know, but it can't be helped." She shrugged.

"First thing tomorrow then?"

"Yeah. I'll meet you here at eight thirty."

I agreed, but I didn't want to wait, so I decided to go visiting on my own. I watched Kate drive out of the parking lot, then I called Amanda and told her I was going to be late.

"Fine, but where are you going and how long will you be?" she asked.

"Not long, I hope. I'm just going to do a little schnauzing around, see what I can dig up."

"Hmm. Well, be careful. Don't get into any trouble."

"Who me? When did I ever?"

"Oh lordy. When did you ever not?"

I grinned to myself, told her goodbye, and punched the first address into the GPS.

***

The first shop was north of town on Lee Highway. It was just after six when I arrived, but the manager had already left for the evening, leaving the lady behind the desk in charge.

I asked if I could look around the shop. She said I could, and so I did. All three service bays were occupied and I could see at least two men working in the pit—performing oil changes, I supposed. I went back to the reception area and asked the woman there a couple more questions, but I didn't get much out of her. She'd worked there for a little over twelve months but couldn't remember ever seeing the owner's truck on the property. I asked her if she knew who might have that information and she gave me the name of the service manager at the East Ridge location on Ringgold Road.

By the time I made it over there it was almost seven o'clock, and the manager, Charlie, was getting ready to close for the night.

His location was a lot like the one I'd just visited; those places are built to one universal design, with an office, a customer waiting area, and three service bays.

"So you guys have just the three lube shops?" I asked him after he'd given me the grand tour.

"Yeah, just the three: this one, the one on Lee Highway, and another on Gunbarrel. Well, there's actually another one on Rossville Boulevard, but it's been closed for years. Bad neighborhood, that. From what I understand we had a series of break-ins—robberies—so Mrs. Greenwood decided it wasn't worth the hassle, much less the danger to the staff, and she decided to close it. That was… oh, I don't know… eight, ten years ago. They tried to sell the property, but couldn't get the price they wanted, so…."

"And where exactly is it?" I asked. *Maybe, just maybe,* I thought.

He told me. I thanked him, and left him to close up.

I sat in the Beast for a minute, thinking. I knew that by the time I got there, the Gunbarrel Road shop would be closed for the night, but I'd already figured it would be a waste of time. On the other hand….

I punched in the address of the Rossville Boulevard location into the GPS, put the car into drive, and eased out onto Ringgold Road. I headed west, and took the ramp on Westside Drive up onto I-24, heading northwest to Rossville Boulevard, where I made the exit and turned south.

I drove slowly, looking for the lube shop. I found it some three fourths of a mile or so from the I-24 exit, set back from the street some fifty yards and surrounded by an asphalt parking lot that stretched all the way to the road. It was so far from the road it was in shadow. If I hadn't been looking for it, I might not have seen it.

On the left side of the building I could see what must once have been the office or customer reception area; the windows were boarded up. To the right of that were three large, overhead roller doors, all closed—the service bays.

I parked my car on the right side of the building, close to the wall, and got out and looked around. The place was in bad shape. There hadn't been a business there for more than ten years, and the state of desolation more than confirmed it.

I walked slowly around to the back. That area too was in total disrepair. The colorful paintwork on the brick walls had long since faded. Even the graffiti had faded.

There were three more huge overhead doors at the rear, but no rear exit door. As far as I could tell, there was no one inside. What few windows there were had been painted over on the inside and boarded up on the outside. I peered through a gap between the boards and the frame, but could see no lights on inside. I rounded the end of the building and looked around. The streetlights on Rossville Boulevard were aided by the lights of several nearby businesses: a "We Tote The Note" used car dealership, a check cashing business, still open, and a convenience store, also open. The brightly lit sign above the huge windows proclaimed it to be a SETO One Stop convenience store, but for some reason that didn't register with me at the time. I did, however, notice the black Mercedes E Class parked in front of it.

Hmmm. I wonder....

I headed around the east end of the building and made my way to the front door. The original door had been replaced with one made of sheet steel. An open padlock hung from the hasp. I pushed, and the door swung silently inward; the hinges had recently been oiled.

This is not good.

I stepped inside what I knew must once have been the front desk area. It was vacant, and from the state of the interior it had been for years—no furniture, just a heap of trash in one corner and a large safe set against the back wall. The safe was open, and I could see that it was empty—no drawers, no shelves, nothing. Everything that could have been stolen had been.

I looked around. To the right, a half-open door gave way to the three service bays. I pushed it open and stepped through. The bays too had been plundered. All that remained were a few empty beer cans and several piles of garbage.

The service bay to the far right was occupied by an old, pale green Chevy Silverado.

Oh yeah. This is it. The son of a bitch must be hiding somewhere.

The service bay closest to me was vacant, revealing the pit below. I'd been in a lube shop before, and I knew that the three pits were actually one, a huge, low-ceilinged room, a concrete bunker below the service bays that housed the pumping equipment and oil supplies. The only access to the pit was a flight of iron stairs just inside the door to my left. I took a step forward, glanced down the stairs.

Shit! There's a light on down there.

I looked around, searching for an escape route should I need one. The six steel roller doors—three at the front and three at the rear of the service bay—were so old they were hand operated. Unfortunately, with the exception of bay three, the chains that raised and lowered them had been removed and were lying in neat piles by their respective doors. The doors could not be opened. The one with its chains intact, the same one with the Chevy in it, was secured by a large steel padlock. That left only the steel door through which I'd entered the building.

Make the call, Harry. Get some backup.

So I did. I called Bob. "Please leave a…."

I hung up and called Kate. Her phone too went straight to voicemail.

Damn! If he has her down there….

"Come on down, Harry. I've been expecting you."

Harry? We're on first name terms now?

I only had to hear the voice to know it was Greenwood.

I slid the VP9 out of its holster. I didn't need to rack it. I always kept one in the chamber.

I took another step toward the stairs and put my free hand on the rail. I stopped, stood still, the hairs on the back of my neck bristling.

"How clever of you to find me. Well, not really. My service manager, Charlie, called me and told me about your conversation. I had an idea you'd drop by. Now do come on down. If you don't, I'm afraid I'll have to hurt this young lady—and please, don't try anything heroic. My gun has a hair trigger."

So she's still alive; that's good.

"Okay," I said. "I'm coming. Don't do anything stupid." I slid the VP9 under my belt at the small of my back and stepped down the stairs.

He was standing against the far wall, in the shadows thrown by the dim light of a small LED lantern. The girl was seated in front of him, taped to a folding steel chair. Her eyes and mouth were taped shut; her cheeks bulged with terror.

And no wonder. He was holding a pistol. It was either a Mark 3 or Mark IV Ruger semi-automatic, a twenty-two, but as Doug Marcaida would say, "It will keel."

I shook my head—not for his benefit, but for mine. I was frustrated because I was in the dead zone: too close for him to miss, and too far away to for me to make a grab for the gun.

"Your gun, Harry. Place it on the floor, carefully, and slide it over to me."

I didn't move. Just stood there, stared at him.

He sighed dramatically. "Now, Harry. Do it now." The barrel of the twenty-two twitched.

I took the VP9 from my waistband and did as he asked. He kicked the gun, sending it skidding away into the dark.

"Now the other, please. I think you Americans call it an ankle piece."

I reached down and slid the Glock 43 from its holster and slid it toward him. It joined the VP9 in the darkness.

He pointed his gun in my direction. "Now, please remove your recording devices."

"I'm not wearing a wire, Greenwood."

"No. Of course you're not," he said sarcastically. "Your phone, please, Harry." He held out his hand. "Just toss it to me."

I did as he asked. I tossed the phone to him, but just far enough away from him for him to take his eyes off me and stretch for it. He did neither. The gun didn't waver. The phone dropped to the concrete floor. I heard the glass crack.

"Really, Harry? Did you think I'd fall for that old trick? You've been watching too many movies." He stepped sideways, hammered the heel of his shoe down on the phone once, twice, three times, and then ground it into concrete. "There. That's much better. Take off your shirt and pants please."

I was starting not to like what was happening. I knew I could take him even if he managed to put one in me, so long as he didn't put it in my head, but he now had the gun to the girl's head. If he pulled the trigger, she was dead, and he would still be able to nail me before I could get to him.

"Do it, Harry," he growled.

Reluctantly, I slipped my shirt off over my head, then removed my shoes, then my pants, leaving me in boxers and my watch and nothing else.

"Hands above your head. Good. Now turn around, slowly. Hmmm. Really? No wire!"

I lowered my arms and turned to face him, my hands hanging loose at my sides. I looked relaxed, but inside I was a coiled spring.

"This is my latest." He glanced down at the girl. "She's hoping you're here to rescue her, aren't you, my dear?"

She shuddered, and then kept shuddering.

"Well it's a nice thought, but it's not going to happen."

"You are one crazy son of a bitch," I said quietly. "But it's over. Lieutenant Gazzara knows I'm here.

Look, I know your beef is with me, okay? You've won. I'm here. Let her go."

"You know, Harry, you're right. But it's not 'beef.' You were more of a challenge. As I mentioned before, I've been following your career. You are a hell of a detective, as your presence here proves. I really hadn't planned on any of this. You were right. I was continuing my research.... And then, when I heard that the police had brought you on, I was delighted. It was an opportunity I couldn't resist. So I decided to put you to the test. Could I best the great detective? The answer, obviously, was a resounding yes."

I was stunned almost speechless. "You're telling me that the reason you killed these girls was to, was to...."

"Well, yes... and no. Just Chloe and..." he glanced down at the girl, "this one. Whatever your name is, dear. No, Harry, you weren't a part of the investigation until after I'd finished with Maggie Hart. That one *was* indeed part of my research. But then you came along. Now I'm going to kill you both." Again, he glanced down at the terrified girl.

"Jesus," I said. "You are one screwed up crazy bastard. You're not going to get away with killing us. It's over. Give it up."

He cackled, then said, "Oh, I don't know. With you and the girl here gone along with truck—" he twitched his head in the direction of opening that gave access to the underside of the old Chevy "—

there will be no way to prove anything. After all, your own father is my alibi for Chloe's abduction. And no one saw me grab this young lady, did they my dear, not even you. Oh, you can't talk can you? You're all tied up, literally!"

"How the hell do you think you're going to pull that off?"

"Oh, that's the easy part," he said, a huge grin on his face. "You see these drums?"

I'd already seen them, and I didn't like what I'd seen: I'd counted eight fifty-five-gallon oil drums.

"They are full of waste oil," he continued. "They should have been recycled a long time ago, but here they are. Very convenient. What would happen, do you suppose, if they were to catch fire or, even worse, were caused to explode?"

I didn't answer him. I knew where he was going with it, and I didn't like it one damn bit.

"Now then, Harry. I told you I was a sport. And I really am curious to see if you're as good as they say, so I'm going to give you and the girl a chance. A small one, to be sure, but a chance nonetheless. I always have enjoyed a gamble. Are you up for it?"

I stared at the smiling face, into the ice blue eyes that never wavered. The gun didn't waver either.

"Well, it doesn't matter. You have no choice. These barrels each weigh a little more than five hundred pounds. You're a big man, but I doubt you could move them, and even if you could, it wouldn't do you any good. You see, there are five pounds of C4 explosive packed against the side of one of the drums. Are you impressed, Harry?"

I didn't answer.

"Hmmm. It's hard to tell in this light if you are or not. I'll assume that you are."

He reached into his pocket and brought out a small remote.

"The explosive has a timer on it," he continued. "It's set to five minutes. I'm going to leave you two here, but as I exit the building, I'm going to activate the timer. That done, you'll have two options: either you disarm the bomb, or you try to get out. The roller doors can't be opened. The door out of the office is steel and I'll lock it on my way out. That's it. There is no other way out. The bomb is taped to one of the drums, close to the floor, so good luck with that. Your guns are over there. Maybe you can shoot the lock off, but I doubt it. Any questions, Harry?"

"You are one sick son of a bitch," was all I could come up with.

"Well, so you say. Now, I want you to check your watch, and then raise your hands above your head and turn around, please. And do it slowly. I'll be watching you."

I looked at my watch. It was 9:17. I raised my hands and turned slowly. My brain had kicked into overdrive. *This is my chance to take the cocky bastard.*

And then my head exploded, searing pain and blinding white light washing over me, and I started to fall. The SOB had hit me in the back of the head with his gun.

I dropped to my knees, barely conscious, as the pain washed over me. I cradled my head in my hands.

"Five minutes, Harry," I heard him shout from the top of the stairs. And then all was quiet.

I staggered to my feet. The girl had heard it all and was shaking with fear. *Five minutes?* I could barely think.

All the same, I lurched over to the girl. *Duct tape! Wrapped tight. Shit. It's too tough to tear.*

I looked wildly around in the dim light. I spotted three empty beer bottles on a ledge under the center service bay. I grabbed one, smashed it and, holding it by its neck, sawed at the tape holding her hands to the chair.

Shit, shit, shit. This is taking way too long.

Finally I had her hands loose, and she started tearing at the tape around her mouth, but to no avail. It was wrapped around her head. I started work on the left leg, then the right. Then I had her free. I looked at my watch.

Oh shit. One minute twenty-eight seconds. What? What? Okay, got it.

I grabbed the girl around the waist, slung her over my shoulder, and ran up the stairs. I dumped her on her feet by the office door, turned, grabbed one of the door chains, wrapped it around my wrist, and pulled. With my other hand, I grabbed her by the arm and pushed her across the office, dragging the chain behind me, yards and yards of it. I shoved her into the safe, wrapped the chain around the stem of the wheel, and jammed myself into the safe on top of the girl. It was a tight fit, but we made it. I hauled on the chain. The hinges were stiff, and I mean really stiff, but the door moved. Slowly. I hauled on the chain, and finally it was shut, all but for the thickness of the chain between it and the frame.

No sooner did I have the door closed than there was a brilliant flash of light that seared through the gap and lit up the inside of the safe. The explosion was tremendous. It lifted the safe off the floor and even spun it once or twice… and then we seemed to fall and fall and fall, finally landing hard among rubble that had only seconds before been the front wall of the lube shop. The girl was under me, and she took most of the impact, but she was still conscious at the end of it, bless her.

I tried to push the door open. The damn thing wouldn't move. We were stuck in there. Thank God I'd had the foresight to make sure the door couldn't close completely. If it had…. Well, that just didn't bear thinking about. The poor kid was suffering under 215 pounds of me, but there was nothing I could do. I was on my back, curled up in the fetal position. There was no way to exert pressure on the door without crushing her.

It was less than five minutes after the blast that the first responders arrived. Four minutes and forty-six seconds exactly, actually; I know because I was still wearing my watch. I yelled and shouted. Once they found us, it only took them a minute to lever the door open again.

I climbed out, still wearing only my boxers, then helped Lindsey out. She tried to stand, but collapsed in a heap at my feet, the duct tape still plastered around her head. I watched as the paramedics lifted her onto a gurney and rolled her into an ambulance. I climbed in after them, and held her hand as they gently cut and stripped the tape away from her mouth and eyes. She lost a lot of hair in the process, but overall she looked… alright. Alive.

"Thank you," she croaked, looking at me. "I think I'm in love with you."

At that I had to smile; the kid was traumatized, bruised, and probably broken, but she still had a sense of humor.

I kissed her on the forehead. "I'll come by and see you later, and we'll talk, okay?"

She nodded. "He grabbed me from behind. I never saw his face."

"Don't worry," I said. "I did. I know exactly who he is." I squeezed her hand and climbed down out of the ambulance. They hauled her away to Erlanger, lights flashing and sirens blasting into the night.

I looked around at what had once been the lube shop. It was no more. The concrete bunker below the service bays—and the office, I realized—had shaped the blast upward. The entire building was gone. The oil that had been in the barrels was burning, but not for long. The fire department quickly blanketed it with foam.

The son of a bitch was right. The evidence is all gone, burned, scattered to the wind.

And then I saw what was left of my car. My almost brand-new Camaro ZL1 was almost completely buried under a pile of rubble. *I wonder if it's totaled?* I thought wryly.

"Oh my God!"

I turned in time to see Kate running toward me, followed by a breathless Lonnie.

"Hey, you," I said, backing away.

"What the hell happened here?" Kate all but screeched. "Why are you naked? Where are your clothes? What the hell have you done, Harry Starke?"

I looked down at my lack of clothing, then grinned at her. "Not naked," I said. "Not quite. I'm still wearing boxers. It's… a long story, Kate."

"Oh, I bet it is. Well I have plenty of time. Spill it."

"Not here. Not now. I need to go home. Take a shower, get dressed, grab a stiff drink and… damn it. I'm hungry. We do need to talk though." I turned and looked at the twisted wreck that had once been my sixty-three thousand dollar ZL1. "And I need a ride. How about you drive me home? Lonnie, you can follow. You need to hear this too. By the way—" I nodded in the direction of the smoking pile of rubble "—my H&K and Glock are under that somewhere."

"I'll let them know. Get in the car."

And I did.

Chapter 29

"Oh… *oh….*" Amanda clapped her hands to her mouth when I walked in, virtually naked, followed by Kate, then by Lonnie.

"It's okay," I said, taking her in my arms and squeezing her. "I had a bit of a… how shall I put it? Accident? Yeah, you could call it that." I kissed the tip of her nose and released her.

"These folks need a drink, and so do I; would you mind? I'll be back in a few minutes and then I'll explain."

She nodded, and I went to the bathroom, the shower, and the bedroom, in that order. Twenty minutes later, wearing shorts and a T-shirt, I joined them poolside, where Amanda had a very large scotch waiting for me.

I sat. I sipped. I closed my eyes. I breathed in the cool mountain air. I opened my eyes and looked at each of them in turn. Then I sipped some more, put my glass down on the teak tabletop, and leaned back in my chair. "So. Where would you like me to begin?"

"At the beginning, you ass," Kate said. "Oops, sorry Amanda."

She shrugged. "You know him as well as I do. Ass it is."

"Ladies, ladies," I said, smiling. "How could you, after what I've just been through?"

"What the hell *have* you been through?" Kate snapped.

And so I told them. I began at when I'd left Kate in the police department parking lot, and I ended with her arrival at the wreckage of the lube shop.

They listened without interrupting. When I was done, all three of them were staring at me in open disbelief.

"What?" I asked.

"You," Kate said, "are out of your friggin' gourd. Are you serious? Who the hell d'you think you are? Jack friggin' Reacher?"

"Er… no," I replied. "But it makes a good story. Could even write a book about it I bet, if I wanted to…."

"Oh for God's sake be serious," Amanda said. "She's right. You're out of your mind. What possessed you to go there alone, much less enter the building without backup?"

"Yes," Kate asked. "Why? Why couldn't you wait until morning like we agreed?"

"I called you, Kate, but you didn't answer. I also called Bob. He didn't answer either. And then Greenwood hollered at me from the pit. He had that kid down there. I had no choice. I was worried sick what he would do to her if I didn't do as he said. How did the date go, by the way?" I grinned at her.

"Date? What date? I was…." She glanced sideways at Lonnie. Lonnie looked down at the floor.

"Oh no," I said. "Not you two. That's just too much."

"Screw you, Harry," Lonnie said, glancing sideways at Kate. She very pointedly ignored him.

"Harry." Amanda grabbed my arm. "You have to stop this—this—you have to stop. You're going to be a…." She realized what she was about say, and caught herself, but not soon enough.

"Amanda," Kate said, her eyes wide. "You're not…. You *are!* You're *pregnant.*"

Oh hell. Here we go.

Amanda didn't answer. She looked at me, her eyes pleading. I shrugged.

"Well?" Kate asked. "Are you? Tell us, for Pete's sake."

Amanda sighed, closed her eyes, and nodded. "Just a little bit."

"A little bit? What the hell does that mean? You either are or you aren't."

"Five weeks."

"Oh, *my* God. *Wow….*"

"Harry," Lonnie said, grinning. "Congratulations, you sneaky bastard. I never thought you had it in you. You too, Amanda…. Not the had it in you bit. I figured you probably did, the congratulations bit. Ah hell."

He stood up, walked around the table, leaned over her, and kissed her full on the lips. She was so surprised she almost fell off the chair, and then she started laughing fit to burst.

"I've been wanting to do that ever since I first met you," he said, and then walked around the table to me.

"Hey," I said, laughing, putting up my hands to ward him off, "we ain't that good of friends."

He stuck out his hand. "I mean it, Harry. I know we didn't always.... Well, congratulations."

I took his hand and shook it. "Thanks, Lonnie. I appreciate it."

"Why didn't you tell us?" Kate demanded.

"We were going to," Amanda said. "When the time was right."

"Wow." Kate was staring at me in a way that made me wonder just what was going through her mind, and then I realized I probably didn't want to know.

"Okay," I said. "That's enough. Let's get back to the matter at hand. Professor Greenwood.

"I'd say that just about all the evidence went up in smoke along with the building, the truck, and my car, and Lindsey said she didn't see his face."

"So it's just your word against his, and you went through all that for nothing."

"Well, not quite. Lindsey did hear it all. And I may have a little surprise…. I think we have enough to arrest him, but I'm not ready just yet."

"How so?" Lonnie asked.

"It's *not* just your word against his, is it?" Kate asked slowly.

I just smiled at her.

"What? You S.O.B., Harry. What are you holding back?"

"I… don't think he was doing it alone." That got her attention. "I think he had an accomplice."

They all stared at me.

"Think about it," I said. "He used August as an alibi. We know that's absolute gold, so he couldn't have abducted Chloe. That means someone else did."

I looked around the group. "Any ideas, anyone?"

"Could he have been working with one of our suspects?" Lonnie asked. "Lister has a Rogue. It could have been him."

"I had the same thought, but it doesn't quite gel. Lister is an idiot. Greenwood is an elitist—and a nut job. I don't think he'd stoop that low. If what I have in mind doesn't fly, it might be worth checking out, but we do need to go and grab Greenwood. Just not tonight. I'm hurting all over. I have a feeling my arm may be broken again. Anyway, Greenwood's not going anywhere. He thinks I'm dead, that he's home free. And you, Kate, don't have probable cause. So let's put that on the agenda for first thing tomorrow morning."

It was almost midnight when they left. I hadn't lied; I had bruises all over my body, and I *was* hurting, especially my barely healed arm. I fell into bed and slept the sleep of the dead. It was the first time I didn't dream in almost a month. I had no visitors, and the beast of my childhood didn't put in an appearance either. In fact, I didn't wake until Amanda shook me.

I looked at the clock. It was almost seven. "What the…."

"I turned the alarm off. You needed the sleep. Here, drink this."

She handed me the best cup of coffee I'd ever tasted, and I drank it down.

Chapter 30

"Where the hell have you been?" Kate asked when I opened her office door and stepped inside.

"What? It's only nine," I said with a grin.

"Sometimes," she said, "I have real trouble trying to figure out what's going on in your head. I thought you'd be champing at the bit to go get Greenwood."

"Oh I am, and we will," I said. "Where's Lonnie and, what is it you call them, Stop and Go?"

She smiled. "Holtz and Foote. They're around somewhere. Lonnie's in the bathroom. He'll be back."

"Kate. I gotta ask. You and Lonnie?"

"Oh hell, Harry. Hang it up. It was just dinner, okay? Nothing more."

"And how times have you had *just dinner*?"

"A couple of times," she said. "No big deal."

It was at that moment he, the aforementioned Lonnie, stuck his head in the door.

"Ah, you made it, I see. Okay if I come in, or are you still talking about me?"

"We weren't talking about you," Kate said. He smiled, but she continued, "Well, Harry asked where you were, and I told him."

Not quite a lie, but almost.

"Okay," I said. "Enough of this banal banter. I want to get our erstwhile professor—no, Dr. Greenwood—and as quickly as possible, before he decides to run. What has the media had to say about the explosion, by the way? Was I mentioned?"

"Not much about the explosion. Nothing at all about you, or Lindsey," Kate said. "The fire department, Erlanger, and our people have managed to keep the lid on tight. Right now it's down to a gas leak. The story the PR people put out is that they're still trying to wade through the rubble, searching for bodies, or survivors."

"That's good. Now, before we go over there and grab him, I need to spend a little time with Mike Willis. I want to look at that security footage one more time. You up for it?"

They were.

There were only a couple of minutes of video I wanted to look at. I wanted to get a good look at the Nissan Rogue.

I've always thought that every single motor vehicle is unique, that they are as dissimilar as fingerprints. It's been known for more than eighty years that tire impressions, regardless of brand, are unique. Every tire will show a different amount of tread wear, along with hundreds of tiny cuts and nicks. However, not much has been done with the body of the vehicle. Bumper stickers and decals and the like are of little use—they're produced in the thousands, and circumstantial at best.

Dings, scratches, rust spots, and cracked or broken glass, however… well, that's what I was looking for. And we found it.

"There," I said to Mike. "Can you enlarge that section and enhance it?"

He could, and he did.

I waited for him to print it. He handed the 8x10 to me. I looked closely at it, and I smiled. *Maybe,* I thought. *Just maybe.*

I thanked him and then turned to Kate and Lonnie. "Okay, let's go do it. Better get Stop and Go on board, too."

"Well," Lonnie said, "are you going to tell us or what?"

"Or what," I said, smiling at him.

"Jeez. Kate, how the hell do you put up with him?"

She grinned at me. "Sometimes I ask myself that very same question."

Chapter 31

It was exactly eleven o'clock when we arrived at the Greenwood home on Riverview. I now had no car, so we traveled in Kate's unmarked. Lonnie followed in one cruiser, Foote and Holtz in another. I had Kate ask them to stay back and park out of sight of the home.

She and I, though, parked right outside the front door, at the bottom of a short flight of steps that led up to a small porch.

I waited for Lonnie to join us, then thumbed the bell push and stepped back. I was taking no chances. I had my Sig forty-five in my hand by my side, and the safety was off.

"Ah, Mr. Starke," he said, opening the door, his eyes sparkling with amusement. "How lovely. Please, do come in…. Oh, and who do you have with you?" he asked, as Kate and Lonnie stepped into sight. "Oh my! Is that a gun you have in your hand, Mr. Starke? Please, put it away. Guns have no place in this house."

I slid the Sig into the holster under my arm.

"Come," he said, beckoning with his entire arm and hand. "Come on into the kitchen and meet Shari, my wife. Shari, this is Harry Starke. I told you all about him. And Lieutenant Gazzara. And… this is?"

I introduced Lonnie to her.

She was maybe five-three in her heels, with a trim figure, long brown hair, a pretty oval face with a pert nose, and a pair of dark eyes that reminded me of an eagle's.

"Before we begin, Harry—it is all right if I call you Harry?"

I nodded, wondering where the hell he was headed. I soon found out.

"Good. I was wondering if I might I talk to you for a moment in private, Harry?"

I glanced at Kate and shrugged. "Sure. Why not."

"Good. Let's go through into the living room, if you don't mind. Shari, my dear, why don't you get the officers a cup of tea, or something cool, perhaps?"

The living room was a big, airy space with a huge picture window and a cathedral ceiling.

"Please, Harry, won't you sit down?"

So I sat, and waited for him to speak.

"You made it out all right then?" he asked, smiling.

Jeez, this guy is absolutely crazy.

"I thought somehow you might. You are indeed a very resourceful man, Harry. How did you do it? The safe? Yes, of course. There was nothing else, was there? I did worry a little about that. I couldn't lock the damn thing, you see, couldn't even close it. The lock mechanism was broken by ruffians. That really is a bad neighborhood, which is why we closed that franchise. Yes, well done, man. Well done."

I could feel my teeth squeaking with how hard I was clenching them together. I got to my feet. "Let's go and rejoin the others."

"It's only your word against mine, you know. I'll deny it."

"Of course you will, Doctor. Shall we?" I didn't wait for an answer, just walked out of the room and left him staring after me.

"Just why are you here, and with these officers?" he asked as he followed me back into the kitchen.

"I'm here to arrest you for the kidnapping of Lindsey Scott, and the murder of Chloe Sandoval. Sergeant Guest, please read Dr. Greenwood his rights."

Lonnie rose to his feet, but before he could open his mouth:

"*What?*" Greenwod was incredulous. "Stop! What the hell are you talking about? I don't know a Lindsey Scott, much less did I kidnap her."

Oh he was good, but I had him beat.

"My word against yours, wasn't it?" I asked mockingly. I took a small digital recorder from my pocket, held it up so he could see it, and then pressed the *play* button.

His voice started up midsentence.

"—when I heard that the police had brought you in, I was delighted. It was an opportunity I couldn't resist. So I decided to put you to the test. Could I best the great detective? The answer, obviously, was a resounding yes."

My own voice from the recorder: "You're telling me that the reason you killed these girls was to, was to…."

"Well, yes… and no. Just Chloe and…. this one. Whatever your name is, dear. No, Harry, you weren't a part of the investigation until after I'd finished with Maggie Hart. That one *was* indeed part of my research. But then you came along. Now I'm going to kill you both."

I clicked the recorder off.

"And on and on," I told him. "I have the entire conversation, and video too. It shows the whole episode, though the quality isn't that good. The light was way too low, but it's good enough to put you away… forever."

"But… how? I made you strip. You weren't wearing…."

"A wire?" I finished for him. "No. I wasn't. Just this." I held up my arm and showed him my watch. "A gift from the Secret Service," I said. "It's wireless. Sends and receives sound and video up to a quarter mile. The receiver was in the trunk of my car, which was all but destroyed, by the way."

I smiled at him. His face was white.

"So you see, I knew I had you for Lindsey's abduction, and Chloe and Maggie, which you admitted to in the recording… which is more than enough, seeing as how I have video of you standing beside Lindsey with a gun in your hand. But with the truck burned to a crisp and no other physical evidence or witnesses, that was all I had. I couldn't tie you to the murder of Dana Walters. But I did have Emoji, didn't I?"

He smiled, but it was looking a little thin, now.

"I also knew you murdered Chloe Sandoval, but how did you do it? How did you abduct her? That was what was puzzling me. I couldn't get around your alibi. You were with my father when she was abducted for Christ's sake. My friggin' father! That, my friend, was a stroke of genius. No one can be in two places at once. Even with your admission on the recording I still couldn't figure out how you pulled it off." I turned to look at Shari. "And then it hit me. You had an accomplice. Didn't he, Mrs. Greenwood?"

She didn't answer. I looked back at him. Even the thin smile he'd worn was gone.

"It was you who abducted Chloe, wasn't it, Mrs. Greenwood?"

"Oh for God's sake. Don't be ridiculous," she said hotly. "That's the stupidest thing I've ever heard."

"Is it? Is it really? Chloe Sandoval was abducted from the Food City parking lot on Hixson Pike by someone driving a silver, late-model Nissan Rogue. We know that because we have the security tapes from the supermarket. They show her getting into the car at precisely 9:55 that evening. The driver of the Nissan was smart enough, or perhaps stupid enough, to cover the license plate with that idiotic emoji. What the hell was that about, by the way?"

Neither of them replied.

"Well, to continue. While Chloe was being abducted you, Doctor, were busy building your alibi, with my father, no less," I paused, shaking my head in faux disbelief.

"So, as I said—" I turned my attention back to Shari Greenwood "—you drive a red Mercedes sports car, I believe, but you also own a late-model Nissan Rogue, and that's what you used to abduct her. That makes you a coconspirator at best, a murderer to at worst. Which is it? And which of you grabbed Lindsey Scott?"

Shari seemed to hesitate, then said, "There must be at least a thousand silver Rogues in Hamilton County. They are all identical. You can't prove it was mine."

"Ah, but you're wrong. You're right in that there are a lot of them; there are, and all of them are almost identical—'almost' being the operative word. Every one is actually completely unique. A car or truck, van, whatever, is very much like a fingerprint. Each will have one or more distinguishing features: scratches, a chip, a sticker… maybe even a ding?" I smiled at her. “I’d be willing to bet—if I were a betting man, of course—that when we inspect that Rogue of yours, we’ll find this ding on the right rear fender.” I laid the photo down in front of her. “See how nice and defined it is?”

Her face was white. I made a wry face, smiled, and then turned my attention back to the doctor; he was glaring at his wife.

“You stupid cow,” he said. “I told you to use the damned truck.”

“And I told you I couldn’t drive the stupid thing.”

He glared at her, shaking his head.

“It’s over, Doc,” I said. “You’re done. You both are.”

He stared at me then shook his head, resignedly. “Well done, Harry. You really are that good. I didn’t believe it, but here we are. You won.”

I almost laughed at him. “You really are crazy, aren’t you? I mean actually, properly insane?”

“Well, you know what they say: ‘There’s a fine line between insanity and genius.’”

“You think you’re a friggin’ *genius*? Jeez, you’re friggin’ batshit crazy, is what you are. *Wow*!”

“Hah, how cleverly you put it.”

Right then, I wanted nothing more than to get him out of my sight, but I had to know…. “But I need to know, Doctor. How could you do it?" I asked. "How could you snuff them out like they were nothing?"

"Oh come, come," he said. "They *were* nothing. Just a means to an end. My research. They were… guinea pigs. It was no different than squashing a bug."

When I heard that, I was consumed with rage at his offhand temerity, and could barely keep my hands at my sides.

"Research? *Research?* Bullshit. You raped them re*peat*edly. What the hell kind of research is that?"

"You raped them?" Shari Greenwood looked stunned. "How… how could you? We, we, we… you sick bastard…." She trailed off, staring at him, angry and hurt. Greenwood's face was a mask.

I turned to Kate and Lonnie, and said, "I'm not allowed to own handcuffs, so would you guys mind doing the honors?" And so they did.

Chapter 32

That afternoon I gave Channel 7's Charlie Grove his promised exclusive interview. I would have liked for Amanda to do it, but she wouldn't, and I understood.

"Well Harry," he said, "congratulations. You did it again, and you saved Lindsey Scott too,"

"Thank you, Charlie. But you're wrong. It was a team effort by the Chattanooga Police Department, and Lieutenant Gazzara in particular."

He smiled. "Yes, I'm sure they helped…." He looked down at his notes. "So tell our viewers, Harry: How did you know that Greenwood was Emoji?"

I smiled. "He told me."

"Huh? Can you explain what you mean by that?"

"Oh, he didn't come right out and say it, but it was in his interactions with me: body language, his eyes, the way he looked at me, his constant use of double entendre. He thought he was smart, and he was, but his ego was his downfall. He had to win, and he had to know that I knew he'd won. So he made sure I knew it was him. But he overplayed it."

And so it went for another twenty minutes, Charlie asking all the usual stupid questions reports always ask. How did I feel when…? How did I think she felt when….? And so on. And then it was over.

Yes, it was over, but I wasn't over it, not yet. I was consumed by a feeling of intense emptiness. I'd experienced it before, and always at the end of a difficult case. I likened it to a woman who'd just had a baby: post-partum depression. What I was feeling as I walked with Amanda back to her car must have been very much akin to that.

"What's going to happen to them?" she asked as we rounded the bend at Ruby Falls. We were in her car, which was nice enough, but it wasn't the Beast.

"Well, Tennessee still has the death penalty, but I doubt either of them will get that. Life without parole is likely for him. For her? Who knows. With a good defense attorney, she might get a few years. She'll probably play the Svengali card, that she was totally under his influence, and she probably was.

"Hey," I said, as Amanda drove the car into the garage. "How about we take a couple of weeks off and head for the islands? Maybe Captain Walker is free and we could charter the boat. It might be the last chance we get before the…."

She set the parking brake and turned in her seat to face me. "Before the what? Go on, say it."

"Before the baby comes." I squinted at her.

She smiled. "Let's do it."

And we did. Three days later we were on board the *Lady May* heading out from Calypso Key at a fast clip, Walker at the helm and his first mate, Tag, serving drinks: gin and tonic for me, cranberry juice for Amanda.

Where we were going, I had no idea.

"Wherever the wind takes us," I said when Walker asked.

He laughed. "I know just the place." And he did.

Thank you.

Thank you for taking the time to read *Emoji.* If you enjoyed it, please consider telling your friends, or posting a short review on Amazon (just a sentence will do). Word of mouth is an author's best friend and much appreciated. Thank you. —Blair Howard.

Reviews are so very important. I don't have the backing of a major New York publisher. I can't afford to take out ads in magazines and on TV. But you can help get the word out.

To those of my readers who have already posted reviews to this novel and my others, thank you for your past and continued support.

If you have comments or questions, you can contact me by email at blair@blairhoward.com, and you can visit my website, http://www.blairhoward.com.

Join the Blair Howard mailing list and I'll give you the first book in the Harry Starke Series as a gift. For instant access, just click this link and tell me where to send the book: http://dl.bookfunnel.com/j6ztln40hc.

Or you might like to dive in at the deep end and read the rest of the stories. They are available as individual ebooks, paperbacks, or audiobooks. The first nine stories are also available in three box sets:

books 1–3, books 4–6, and books 7–9, all at special reduced prices. Here are the links:

Box Set 1 US: http://amzn.to/294O6RF

Box Set 1 UK: http://amzn.to/2m80TJh

Box Set 2 US: http://amzn.to/2m7TMjM

Box Set 2 UK: http://amzn.to/2lK4NWc

Box Set 3 US: http://bit.ly/harrybooks7-9

Box Set 3 UK: http://bit.ly/harrybooks7-9UK

Book 10 in the series, Calaway Jones, is available here in the US:

https://www.amazon.com/dp/B06XQKFR5Q

And here in the UK:

https://www.amazon.co.uk/dp/B06XQKFR5Q

Made in United States
North Haven, CT
11 June 2023